FROM BAD TO WORSE

"Finally caught ya red-handed, didn't I, girl?" barked Roy Dixon, the mule ears of his high-topped boots bouncing as he strode quickly forward. "Now you two best prepare to meet your *Maker*!"

Fargo moved in front of the girl. "It was me, Dixon. I lured her over here. Leave her out of it."

The pilgrim stopped and snapped the rifle to his shoulder. He grunted sharply. His head snapped back on his shoulders. The rifle sagged in his arms. Stumbling forward, he arched his back, dropped the rifle, and sank to his knees.

He knelt there for a moment, as if praying. Then he fell facedown on the ground.

Fargo leaped to his feet, bounded over the log, and dropped to one knee beside Dixon. Protruding from the man's back, firmly embedded between his shoulder blades, was a Chiricahua tomahawk. . . .

THE TRAILSMAN

#308

BORDER BRAVADOS

by

Jon Sharpe

A SIGNET BOOK

SIGNET
Published by New American Library, a division of
Penguin Group (USA) Inc., 375 Hudson Street,
New York, New York 10014, USA
Penguin Group (Canada), 90 Eglinton Avenue East, Suite 700, Toronto,
Ontario M4P 2Y3, Canada (a division of Pearson Penguin Canada Inc.)
Penguin Books Ltd., 80 Strand, London WC2R 0RL, England
Penguin Ireland, 25 St. Stephen's Green, Dublin 2,
Ireland (a division of Penguin Books Ltd.)
Penguin Group (Australia), 250 Camberwell Road, Camberwell, Victoria 3124,
Australia (a division of Pearson Australia Group Pty. Ltd.)
Penguin Books India Pvt. Ltd., 11 Community Centre, Panchsheel Park,
New Delhi - 110 017, India
Penguin Group (NZ), 67 Apollo Drive, Rosedale, North Shore,
Auckland 1311, New Zealand (a division of Pearson New Zealand Ltd.)
Penguin Books (South Africa) (Pty.) Ltd., 24 Sturdee Avenue,
Rosebank, Johannesburg 2196, South Africa

Penguin Books Ltd., Registered Offices:
80 Strand, London WC2R 0RL, England

First published by Signet, an imprint of New American Library,
a division of Penguin Group (USA) Inc.

First Printing, June 2007
10 9 8 7 6 5 4 3 2 1

The first chapter of this book previously appeared in *Montana Marauders*,
the three hundred seventh volume in this series.

Ⓟ REGISTERED TRADEMARK—MARCA REGISTRADA

Printed in the United States of America

PUBLISHER'S NOTE
This is a work of fiction. Names, characters, places, and incidents either are
the product of the author's imagination or are used fictitiously, and any resem-
blance to actual persons, living or dead, business establishments, events, or
locales is entirely coincidental.

   The publisher does not have any control over and does not assume any
responsibility for author or third-party Web sites or their content.

The Trailsman

Beginnings . . . they bend the tree and they mark the man. Skye Fargo was born when he was eighteen. Terror was his midwife, vengeance his first cry. Killing spawned Skye Fargo, ruthless, cold-blooded murder. Out of the acrid smoke of gunpowder still hanging in the air, he rose, cried out a promise never forgotten.

The Trailsman they began to call him all across the West: searcher, scout, hunter, the man who could see where others only looked, his skills for hire but not his soul, the man who lived each day to the fullest, yet trailed each tomorrow. Skye Fargo, the Trailsman, the seeker who could take the wildness of a land and the wanting of a woman and make them his own.

Southern Arizona, 1859—
if the rattlers and Apaches don't kill you,
then the desperadoes definitely will.

1

The tall, dark rider reined his horse to a sudden halt. Hand flicking to the Colt .44 on his right hip, he squinted his lake blue eyes at the cottonwood copse about fifty yards up the bench on his right.

A large mule deer buck crashed from the serviceberry and wild currant shrubs at the base of the trees, shook his head with annoyance, and loped up a cedar-stippled ridge. Skye Fargo eased his hand away from his Colt's grips as he watched the thick-necked buck, showing a gunpowder gray coat and a six-point rack, heavy with spring velvet, gain the ridge crest and disappear down the other side.

Fargo snorted, relieved, as he stared at the ridge. "Don't worry, old-timer. Your meat's too tough for my palate. I'll wait for something younger and smaller. You have a good summer with plenty of bunchgrass."

Fargo swung around in his saddle, scanning his back trail, one eye squinted against the sun glare. Nothing back there but rocky ridges and cedars, as far as he could tell. But before the buck had startled him, he could have sworn he'd spied a horse-shaped shadow scuttling about that high granite ridge, quartering southwest.

He'd been over and through that country several times today, and he had nothing to show for his jumpiness but a sense that he was being followed . . .

Shuttling his gaze back and forth across the ridge,

he reached for his canteen, popped the cork, and took a pull of the stale water. Beneath him, the Ovaro pinto rippled its withers and blew.

"I know, hoss," Fargo said as he hammered the cork back into the canteen's spout with the heel of his hand, his troubled gaze still quartering over the canyon-split country behind him. "We'll stop soon, and you can have your own drink and a good, long roll." The big, buckskin-clad rider known as the Trailsman took a deep breath and let it out slowly. "Wouldn't mind one of those myself."

Fargo dropped the canteen over the saddle horn and heeled the Ovaro into a walk for several yards, as he continued glancing behind, before urging the magnificent stallion into a trot. A quarter hour later he topped a rise and drew back on the pinto's reins. Below, the five covered wagons of the train he was piloting to a town called Genesis, newly established in Bone Creek Canyon in southern Arizona Territory, lumbered west amidst angling shadows, the dust kicked up by their iron-shod wheels lifting in honey-colored clouds against the copper rocks and boulders on both sides of the trace.

The white canvas covers stretched taut across the ash bows glowed in the soft, westering light. Left of the wagons, a narrow creek meandered against the base of a low sandstone ridge. Above the ridge hung a powder horn moon in the clear desert sky.

Fargo gigged the pinto down the hill. He passed the fifth and fourth wagons. As the pinto moved up to the left front wheel of the third, a voice rose from the driver's box.

"Mr. Fargo!" exclaimed Jasper Felton, a short man with a bib-length, steel-colored beard and a shabby blue bowler on his bald head. He plucked the long yellow foxtail drooping from between his lips. "The missus is growin' mighty wrung out. Can't we stop soon?"

Fargo glanced at the woman sitting beside Felton—a triple-chinned brunette in a poke bonnet, whose loose gray dress and multiple aprons could not conceal the fact that she outweighed her husband by a good sixty pounds. Recently a mail-order bride from Ohio, she was pouty and temperamental, though a fair cook.

"I'm about to discuss the matter with Dixon."

Fargo continued on past the next wagon, blinking against the dust churned up by the heavy wheels, and drew even with the first Pittsburgh. The party's leader, Roy Dixon, sat beside his young wife, Deana. Dixon wore his usual bulldog scowl as he leaned forward over his knees, the ribbons of his four-mule hitch in his hands.

Dixon was heading up the party of merchants from Hutchinson, Kansas, to Genesis. Because of its close proximity to planned railroad lines, gold country, and freight trails into Mexico, Genesis was expected to grow as large as Albuquerque in the next ten years.

"Where the hell you been?" Dixon snapped when his eyes found Fargo. "I thought you were supposed to be scoutin' the trail *ahead*. Ain't that why we hired you? Hellfire, with all these blasted washes and Mexican traders' trails out here, we mighta taken a wrong turn and taken the Devil's good time to get back on track!"

Biting his tongue, Fargo pointed ahead, where the creosote-stippled desert rose up against the ridge on the other side of the creek. The ridge flanked the area on three sides, offering protection from all directions but north. "We're gonna stop in that horseshoe of the creek for the night. There's a ford about a mile ahead."

Dixon's goat-whiskered, gray-eyed face blossomed with anger. "We ain't stoppin' till we get to Genesis! We're almost there, dang blast it!"

Being a religious man—all five wagons were composed of Lutherans who not only intended to establish

3

their own businesses in Genesis, but a Lutheran church, as well—Dixon did not take the Lord's name in vain. That didn't keep him from shooting his mouth off in fine, fire-and-brimstone fashion, however.

Fargo had been humoring the belligerent Bible-thumper for the past three weeks, and he looked forward to unloading the man and his wife, pretty as she was, in Genesis. In fact, he thought he'd probably earned a spot in heaven for not drilling a .44 round through the Lutheran's broad forehead . . . yet.

"Earlier, I thought we could make it today," Fargo said, deftly stitching patience into his voice while staring straight ahead. "But that was before I got a whiff of men on our trail. Besides that, Mrs. Felton's feelin' poorly. We'll stop while we still have enough light to set up camp."

"Hold up there!" Dixon shouted as Fargo pressed his heels to the pinto's flanks. "Time is money, Fargo, and I want to get to Genesis tonight and—" Dixon broke off the tirade, the muscles in his craggy face planing out. "What's that about men on our trail?"

"Last few hours, someone's been foggin' us." He glanced over his shoulder. "I haven't cut any sign, but my sniffer rarely lies . . ."

"What do you suppose they're after, Mr. Fargo?" Mrs. Dixon asked, breathless.

Fargo was happy to have an excuse to shuttle his gaze to the woman. Girl, actually. Fargo didn't think she was a day over twenty. Another mail-order bride, he suspected, though Dixon was tight-lipped about his wife and, being the proprietary type, kept her bound to her cook pots and water buckets, raising his hackles at any man who gave her more than a passing glance. Fargo had known mules treated better than she.

With gold-blond hair, brown eyes, and delicate features, she was a high-bred filly if he'd ever seen one. Probably from a wealthy family back east that, having fallen on hard times, had married her off to the pious Kansan.

Fargo tried to keep his eyes from her ample bosom, which, he noted in the periphery of his vision, rose and fell sharply, the lightly freckled cleavage opening, the breasts separating, with each inhalation. Her peaches-and-cream cheeks were flushed with worry.

"If they're after anything, it's probably only the mules," Fargo lied.

If whoever was behind them had seen Mrs. Dixon taking her morning ablutions in one of the creeks they'd camped beside, they'd be after more than the mules. Fargo had stumbled upon her once himself, and had felt as though his heart, gripped by the strong fist of lust, had been turned counterclockwise in his chest.

"Nothin' to worry about, ma'am. Like I said, I haven't cut any sign, so it might only be my imagination. Still better to hole up before nightfall, though, than to continue in the dark. And, like I said, Mrs. Felton's feelin' poorly."

"You will stay *close*, though, won't you, Mr. Fargo?"

Deana Dixon's eyes were riveted on the Trailsman, one hand spread open on her heaving bosom. Her eyes flicked across the Trailsman's fringed buckskin tunic, drawn taut across the iron-hard slabs of his chest.

For a moment, the girl appeared a little faint. Then, her face turning crimson, she looked at her husband, who was scowling at her incredulously. "I mean, he's so well *armed* and all. . . ."

"Don't worry, dear," Dixon growled, clamping his heel down on the two-bore express gun beneath his seat. "I've got old Henrietta here, remember? Not too many men can get past her. Besides"—he canted his head at the girl and winked—"I think Mr. Fargo might be a little trail-addled. I've got keen eyes and ears, too, and I haven't seen or heard anything out of the ordinary."

"That may be true, Dixon," Fargo said, reining his horse in a circle and gesturing for the other wagons to follow him. "But this party will be camping against that ridge this evenin', and that includes your wife. If you want to risk *your* life, that's your business. But I won't let you risk *her* life, as well."

Fargo didn't turn his glance to Dixon's outraged face. Instead, he neck-reined the pinto westward and gigged the horse into an instant, ground-eating lope. A hundred yards ahead, he crossed the creek and scouted the horseshoe of shoreline rising to the ridge base and carpeted in lush, green grass—mostly grama grass and bluestem, with a sprinkling of tarbrush and catclaw. From the base of the crenellated rock wall behind him, he could see a broad swath of chaparral in three directions.

He sat the pinto, staring at the wagons strung out in a line along the opposite shore. Roy Dixon glared at him from his driver's box, his young wife beside him, both rocking with the wagon's sway. As Dixon approached the ford, he cursed and swung his mules toward the creek.

Fargo smiled and poked his broad-brimmed hat off his forehead. Dixon's team splashed through the water, the wagon following, bouncing sharply as the wheels clattered and barked across the rocks.

The Trailsman waited, watching the other wagons, pleased to see that the second wagon, a heavy-axled freighter driven by the dentist and blacksmith, Merlin Haggelthorpe, didn't ford until Felton's Conestoga was lumbering through the grass toward Fargo. No more than two wagons in a stream at the same time, in case one had trouble and needed assistance.

When all the wagons were safely across, Fargo directed the drivers to line up along the shore. Fargo rode up and down the line, giving orders and suggestions. When the wagons were situated and the men were unhitching the teams, Fargo rode back across the creek and galloped west. He wanted to give the country around them a thorough going-over before dark.

It was Chiricahua country, after all.

Finding little except a herd of mule deer grazing a broad, grassy table two miles northwest, Fargo brought one down with a single shot from his Henry and headed back the way he'd come. It was fully dark now, the sky like black velvet upon which a handful of silver dust had been tossed.

Fargo splashed across the creek and turned the horse between two wagons. The pilgrims had built a large cook fire. The men were sitting around drinking coffee and mending harness while the women hauled water from the creek and prepared supper, pots clattering and kindling snapping, mesquite smoke perfuming the air.

Fargo shoved the field-dressed deer off the back of his horse. It landed with a thud near the fire. The men closed around to look at the fresh meat, their eyes bright with eager anticipation.

They'd run out of fresh game two nights ago, and, since they'd been in Apache country, Fargo hadn't wanted to trigger a shot.

"It's small," he told Mrs. Haggelthorpe, a pale, doughy woman in a burlap dress and apron peeling potatoes near her husband's rickety folding chair. "It should last us till we get to Genesis, though."

"Nice, Mr. Fargo," intoned Jasper Felton, a mule collar draped over his left shoulder, a stout needle in his right hand. "Very nice indeed!"

Fargo began to turn away when he saw a slender figure standing in the shadows off his left stirrup. A pale hand extended a steaming tin cup. "Coffee, Mr. Fargo?"

Deana Dixon's doe-eyed gaze met his. Was she intentionally revealing more cleavage than usual, or was it just his imagination?

Fargo took the cup in his left hand. "Obliged."

"Will you be joining us this evening?" she asked with a wry arch of her brow. "Or is the lone wolf going to tend his own fire again, as usual?"

"I'll be campin' downstream. I can—"

"Yes, I know," said Deana Dixon, her full lips stretching back from her white teeth, brown eyes glinting reflected firelight. "You can see and hear better when you're away from the group."

Fargo found his glance dropping to her bosom, the lace-edged bodice rising and falling slowly, the scalloped lace stretching away from her deep cleavage. It had been a long trip, and he hadn't had a woman in a couple of weeks, but he kept a short leash on his lust.

His own personal rules didn't allow for cavorting with the women in his charge. Sleeping with any woman in a wagon train, least of all a married woman, was akin to hoorawing a herd of bull buffalo with calves.

Fargo raised the cup. "Thanks for the coffee." He pinched his hat brim and glanced toward the fire, his gaze picking out Roy Dixon down on his knees as he and Ben Leonard, an assayer whose wife, Clara, intended to open a haberdashery in Genesis, conferred over a cracked wagon brake Felton held in his hands.

Fargo glanced once more at Deana Dixon on the other side of his horse, smiling obliquely up at him.

He booted the pinto toward the creek.

2

Fargo spent the next hour walking up and down the stream, watching for any sign of interlopers. Several times he ventured a hundred or so yards from the water's tinny murmur, relying on his frontiersman's sharp hearing to warn him of danger.

He neither heard nor saw anything unusual.

Why was it, then, that the hair on the back of his neck refused to stop pricking?

He hopscotched the creek ford and squatted down beside his cook fire a good sixty yards downstream from the others. He poured a cup of coffee, set the percolator on a flat rock at the edge of the ring, and added another log to the low flames.

As the pine sap snapped and sizzled, Fargo moved back away from the fire, strode into an aspen copse, and hiked a hip on a mossy boulder. He didn't want to stay too close to the fire and lose his night vision, or make himself an easy target to whomever or whatever his senses told him was stalking around out there in the dark.

Soon he'd head over to the pilgrims' fire, fill a supper plate, and make sure the men were keeping their lookout schedule. Weary travelers had been known to get careless on their last night in the wild, and end up losing their topknots.

He froze suddenly, a half-built cigarette stretched between the thumb and index fingers of both hands.

He'd heard something. There it was again: footfalls in deep grass.

The Trailsman shoved the tobacco and cigarette paper back into their hide pouch, returned it to his shirt pocket, and lifted his Henry. Softly, so that the metallic scrape sounded little louder than two reeds rubbing together, he levered a shell into the rifle's breech.

He began moving slowly toward the ridge, setting each foot down silently, sensing as much as seeing each branch, leaf, and rock in his path.

When he was within a few feet of the ridge, he cat-footed along its base, heading west before turning back toward the creek, turning again and striding back toward his own fire.

A silhouette appeared before him. Long hair fluttered around the shoulders. A slender Indian brave. He probably had a hatchet in one hand, a pistol in the other.

Fargo's heart quickened as he raised the rifle. The light breeze wafting against his face was rife with the smell of cherry blossom perfume, talcum, and apple-scented toilet water. A woman.

Fargo lowered the rifle and continued walking toward his camp. Her back to him, Deana Dixon stood in his fire's glow, looking around and softly calling his name.

"Here."

She turned with a start, and his heart skipped a beat. She'd obviously taken a sponge bath. Her skin was clean-scrubbed and beautifully flushed, a few curls of hair strategically arranged about her aristocratic jawline. Her wide mouth, red as ripe apples, was flanked by two perfect dimples.

She wore a black cape with a purple dress. A good outfit to wear in the dark if you didn't want to be seen, say, stealing away from your husband's wagon. . . .

"Sneakin' into a man's bivouac is a good way to get yourself shot."

She raised the oilcloth-covered plate in her hands. "I brought your supper." Wisps of steam rose around the oilcloth, the woman's own breath visible in the cool desert air.

"Obliged," Fargo said, keeping his eyes downcast as he accepted the plate. He walked around the fire, leaned the rifle against a tree, and sat down on a log.

"Do you mind if I stay while you eat?" She added quickly, "I can take your plate back when I go."

Fargo flipped the oilcloth off the steaming meat, potatoes, and canned greens, and draped it across his knee. He picked up the fork and lifted his gaze to the woman still standing on the other side of the fire, her hands fidgeting with the tasseled ends of her cape.

"Your husband know you're here?"

"Of course." She stopped and looked away. "No. He and Mr. Leonard were still working on their brakes." She turned to him with a defiantly arched brow. "Would I need permission to serve your supper, Mr. Fargo?"

Fargo sniffed the steam. "Smells good." He poked his boot toe at the coffeepot. "Help yourself. You'll find an extra cup in my war bag. While you're at it, pour me a cup."

She fished a cup from the canvas war bag, filled both cups, then looked around nervously, finally deciding to sit down on the log beside him.

"Growing chilly," she said when she'd sipped the coffee. She shivered, hunkering low and gazing at the fire as if trying to absorb as much warmth as she could.

Fargo ate purposefully, shoveling the food in one forkful after another of the roasted meat, tender and lightly charred, and the dark gravy spiced with wild onions. He didn't believe in table manners anywhere but at a table. Out here, you ate as much as you could while you could; no telling when you'd get another chance.

"It'll be hotter'n hell in another month," he said around a mouthful of potatoes.

"Is Genesis very high?"

"It's high, and you'll have snow in the winter, but from May to October you'll be able to fry eggs on the rocks."

"I hope I'll get along. It was Mr. Dixon's idea to move west. He believes he can double his capital out here in three years."

Fargo looked at her over the rim of his coffee cup. "Where you from? Not Kansas."

"Maryland."

"What brought you to Kansas?"

"My father was swindled out of his shipping business. Mr. Dixon was a distant relation. His own wife died and"—her voice dropped an octave—"he found himself in the market for another."

"Your folks shipped you off, huh? You must be a good twenty years younger than Dixon."

She looked at him sharply, as if startled by his candor. Her expression softened. "Sixteen."

The conversation meandered into small talk, and then Fargo forked the last bite of meat into his mouth, set the fork and oilcloth on the plate, and held it out to her. "Well, there's your plate, Mrs. Dixon. Much obliged."

She looked at him sharply again, as if she hadn't been expecting him to finish so fast. Small lines formed over the bridge of her fine, straight nose. Her lips moved, but no words came out.

"No hurry, I reckon," Fargo grunted.

He dropped the plate in the dust, slid over to her, grabbed her to him, and pressed his mouth to hers. She gave a little, indignant grunt and a halfhearted jerk. But then her lips opened slowly. Her tongue entangled with his, and the tension left her arms and shoulders.

Just as she began to melt in his arms, leaning into him for more, she pulled back. Her eyes flashed angrily. She brought her right hand back and then swung it forward against his cheek with a resolute, stinging smack.

She leaped to her feet, crossing her arms on her chest and balling the cape in her fists. "What do you think you're doing?"

Fargo stood before her. "Giving you what you came for. I don't normally oblige women in my wagon party, but since your husband's a jackass, and you obviously need it as bad as I do, I'm willing to make an exception. We best be quiet, though. I need to keep my ears skinned."

"What on earth are you talking about?"

Fargo wrapped his arms around her. She squirmed and gave a few light kicks as he pressed his hands firmly against her bottom and pulled her dress up around her waist.

Holding the dress up with one hand, he spread his other hand across her bare left butt cheek. A nice little rump—smooth-skinned, firm, and well-rounded. Her thigh was finely tuned and muscled. She'd probably ridden Daddy's horses back east, and no doubt drove the stable boys crazy. She was probably the most spirited filly in the barn, as a matter of fact.

"You always go around without underwear, Mrs. Dixon? And on a chilly night like this?"

"How dare you! I'm going to scream."

"Enough games, or I'll send you back to your wagon."

"You're mad."

"Am I?"

Fargo dropped the dress and ran his hands up beneath the cape. He splayed his fingers across the bare, hot skin of her back, pressing the tips against the delicate spine as he slid them up toward her shoulders then across her ribs and around to her chest. She sucked a sharp breath as he pressed both palms around her full breasts, jutting nipples prodding his palms like rubber nubbins as he squeezed.

"No corset, either. Not even a chemise."

She leaned her head back on her shoulders, eyes closed. She was breathing sharply, enjoying his touch. "Please, Mr. Fargo. Don't think ill of me. I've tried to love him, but Mr. Dixon is a cold man, and . . ."

Fargo was kneading her breasts, pinching her nipples. "An *old* man, too. Probably not all that capable any longer of satisfying a beautiful woman the way she ought to be satisfied."

"Do you think me awful?" She wrapped her arms around his shoulders, not waiting for his answer. "I can't help myself!"

"I reckon we're in the same boat, then."

Fargo picked her up in his arms and, looking cautiously around, carried her into the paloverdes. Earlier, he'd spied leaves banked a good two feet deep against a fallen log. He looked around for the bed as she nuzzled his neck and nibbled his earlobes.

"We gotta do this quiet-like. No noise, understand?"

She nodded against his neck, her hair tickling him.

He should have been horsewhipped for what he was about to do, especially with marauders possibly lurking around.

Fargo laid her down in the leaves and knelt between her spread legs. He unbuckled his cartridge belt. As he laid the belt over the log, with the gun butt in easy reach, she rose to a sitting position and began unbuttoning his buckskins. Her breath rose sharply, puffing in the cold air.

When she'd peeled his buckskins down his thighs, she opened the fly of his long johns. His shaft sprang out like a snake striking from its hole. She cooed and took the creature in both hands, caressed it as if to tame it, then ran her tongue over the bulging head.

Fargo swept her hair back from her cheeks, staggering slightly as an icy bolt of pleasure lanced his loins. He croaked, "Jesus."

She slid farther down, taking his shaft deep into her mouth and down her throat. She sucked on it, breathing through her nose. The night pitched dreamily around them as her throat opened and closed around the swollen tip. He was biting his cheek, holding himself back, as she lifted her head and lay back in the leaves.

Fargo crabbed forward on his knees, lifted her dress to her waist, her cape to her neck, and slid the shaft home without any effort at all.

She was ready.

It wasn't long before her long legs were wrapped around his back and she was bucking up against him. She clawed his back and kneaded his shoulders, several times lifting her head to run her tongue across his chest, to nibble his bulging muscles.

As he propped himself on his arms and rose up on his boot toes, driving deep, her mouth flew open suddenly, and he clamped his hand across her lips, muffling her scream as they both came at once.

He sagged on top of her and they lay for a while, breathing hard.

"Come on," she said, scrubbing her hands through his hair, tugging brusquely on his ears. "Out of your clothes."

Fargo shook his head and rose onto his arms, staring down at her. Her heavy, upturned breasts lolled against her chest, the nipples still erect. Her brown eyes flashed in the starlight.

"Gotta keep watch," he growled. "Can't go gallivantin' around in the raw."

"We're safe," she whispered. "I haven't heard a

15

thing, and I'm sure Roy's still playing with his brakes." Chuckling, she reached up and began unbuttoning his shirt. "I wanna see you naked, Skye."

He shook his head. "Out of the question."

She sat up and tossed the cape over her head. The bone clip had long since fallen out of her hair, and the entire gold-blond mass swirled around her shoulders and breasts. She cut such a bewitching figure, lying there in the leaves, one raised knee bent toward the other, that he felt his rod stiffening again.

He stood, looked around, then began removing his shirt. He was acting like a shaver with a woody for the schoolmistress, but he couldn't help himself. When he'd tossed the buckskin tunic over the log, he kicked off his boots. She lay before him, propped on her elbows, watching as he stumbled out of his rumpled jeans, long johns, and socks.

He stood over her, the cold air feeling good against his skin, which was sweat-slick from the fire of his lust. His shaft standing nearly straight up and throbbing, he dropped again to his knees. He crouched to place a lingering kiss on each of her coltish legs, and she shuddered as he ran his hands up and down her thighs.

Gently, he spread her legs, the leaves rustling beneath her.

"Wait." She scrambled onto her hands and knees, faced the log and the dying fire beyond, and grabbed a couple of the log's stubby branches for support.

She tested her grip, then wagged her fanny at him and giggled. "Okay."

Fargo glanced around again, listening. No sounds but occasional pops and snaps from the fire ring and the constant, low rush of the creek.

"All right," he said, turning to her and taking her hips in his hands. "But this is the last time . . ."

She laughed. "Sure it is." She squealed the last word as he slid himself home and, holding her tightly before him, began thrusting.

16

Skye Fargo had slept with his share of women. Some would say more than his share. But there was something about the way this girl clutched him deep inside her, the way her body molded to his hands, the way she moved, ramming her bottom against him, in perfect sync with his own lunges, that made him feel he'd entered a whole new world.

Somehow, he managed not to throw his head back and howl, wolflike, as, after about five minutes of blissful, savage mating, he emptied his loins deep inside her. It took a long time to empty the barrel, and there were more than the usual minidetonations after the main explosion—so many, in fact, that he thought his knees would give out before his dong did.

Exhausted, sweat trickling into his eyes, he squeezed her hips and began backing away. Her head had been sagging between her shoulders as she maintained her hold on the branch stubs. Now she lifted her head, tossing her hair away from her eyes.

She froze, then gave a clipped, startled cry.

Fargo followed her gaze in the direction of his camp. A stocky figure in a bulky coat and floppy-brimmed hat moved toward them, rifle extended straight out from his chest.

Still half inside the girl, Fargo froze.

"Finally caught ya red-handed, didn't I, girl?" barked Roy Dixon, the mule ears of his high-topped boots bouncing as he strode quickly forward. "Now you two best prepare to meet your *Maker*!"

Fargo slid off the girl and, looking around for his guns but knowing he wouldn't reach either in time, did as Dixon had suggested. "It was all me, Dixon. I lured her over here. Leave her out of it."

The pilgrim stopped and snapped the rifle to his shoulder. He grunted sharply. His head snapped back on his shoulders. The rifle sagged in his arms. Stumbling forward, he arched his back, dropped the rifle, and sank to his knees.

3

A woman screamed up the wash and Fargo raked his eyes from the tomahawk protruding from Roy Dixon's back to stare into the darkness toward the pilgrims' camp.

Quiet footsteps sounded to his left. "Oh, my God!" Fargo turned as Deana Dixon, feebly covering herself with her dress wadded in both hands, stood ten feet away, staring down at her dead husband. She opened her mouth to scream, but Fargo lunged toward her and clamped one hand over her mouth as several shots and yells sounded behind him.

"Quiet as a church mouse, hightail it into the brush and stay there until I say it's safe to come out." He kept his hand over her mouth and stared into her horrified eyes. "Understand?"

Her lips quivered under his hand, and he could feel her hot breath against his palm. Her eyes cleared slightly. She nodded.

He released her as several more shots and yells rang out from the pilgrims' camp. She turned and, casting doubtful glances behind her, began running back in the direction she'd come from.

Fargo scrambled into his boots and hat, and, heedless of being otherwise naked, knowing there was no time to dress if he was going to save the wagon train from a massacre, sprinted along the wash's sandy bank. Holding the Henry rifle in both sweaty hands, his heart somersaulting in his chest, he traced a long bend in the wash through which a thin stream of water trickled.

Rifle and pistol shots rose on his left. Women screamed. Men shouted in English and Spanish.

Spanish?

Fargo had slowed to turn up the bank on his left when the sound of snapping brambles sounded ahead. He stopped and looked up the wash as a figure materialized out of the brush along the bank, bolting into the wash, stones rattling and clacking under the man's boots, his spurs chinging.

"Madre Maria!" the man cried.

The shadow dropped to the floor of the wash with a soft splash, water glistening like quicksilver in the starlight.

Fargo bounded forward, extending the Henry straight out from his right hip. He saw the shape of a broad sombrero as the man's head turned toward him.

"Hold it!" Fargo raked out.

The man leaped to his feet and staggered to the other side of the stream. Right of his silhouette, a silver barrel winked. There was a flash and a pistol crack.

The slug whistled past Fargo's right ear and snapped a branch behind him. A half second later, Fargo squeezed the Henry's trigger. The report melded with several others ahead and to his left.

The man before him grunted, flew straight back, and landed on the rocks with a raucous *ching* of his spurs. At the same time, two more figures broke from the brush ahead of Fargo and bounded up the wash. They triggered two shots behind them, and Fargo threw himself against the sandy bank as the slugs whistled past him and plunked against the rocks.

When the two figures had fled, Fargo jumped to his feet and ran over to the man he'd shot. The Mexican lay on his back, a bloody hole in his right cheek, another making a bloody puddle of his belly. The man's broad-brimmed sombrero lay smashed in the water beneath his head. He had a full mustache, and two big, bone-handled knives protruded from sheaths on both hips. In his right hand he was still holding a long-barreled Navy Colt revolver, a thin wisp of smoke curling from the end of the barrel.

Fargo didn't take time to wonder why, if their attackers were Mexican, one of them had thrown a Chiricahua tomahawk. Raking a fresh round into his Henry's breech, he ran up the wash, keeping to the sandy right bank to save his feet.

He'd run only twenty yards when he realized the gunfire had died. He ran another fifty yards, tracing the wash's meandering course between cottonwoods, mesquite shrubs, and occasional saguaros silhouetted against the starry sky, when a horse nickered on his right, and a shod hoof rang off a rock.

He stopped, pricking his ears to hear above his heart's thudding.

Men grunted and groaned. Two people were arguing in Spanish and English, though Fargo couldn't hear what they were saying.

A horse whinnied, and hooves thudded.

Fargo sprang up the wash's right bank and, wincing as his right boot clipped a cholla, the "jumping cactus," he zigzagged through brush clumps. Ahead, a bridle chain rattled. Fargo bounded left around a boulder, and stopped.

Ahead, the silhouettes of four horseback riders appeared, moving from his left to his right and heading away through the creosote and mesquite. Fargo snapped the Henry to his shoulder, drew a bead on one of the four diminishing figures silhouetted against the deep purple sky, and fired.

Boom!

A man snarled.

There was the thud of a body hitting the ground. A

horse whinnied shrilly and buck-kicked. Several shots sounded, and Fargo dropped to one knee as the slugs plunked into the ground or trimmed creosote branches ahead of him.

The remaining riders disappeared, and galloping hooves receded into the distance.

There was silence but for the distant cooing of a night bird.

Fargo stood, keeping his ears open, and walked ahead through the prickly desert scrub, setting one foot down gently in front of the other and holding the Henry straight out from his right hip.

The dry, hot desert caliche crunched faintly under his boots. He turned right around a mesquite, then left around a wagon-sized boulder. Pebbles tumbled from atop the boulder, hitting the ground a few feet from Fargo's right foot.

Fargo wheeled.

A stocky figure crouched atop the boulder, a black form against the sky. Long hair hung to the man's shoulders. Fargo smelled the distinctive, gamy smell of the desert Apache—musty leather, rancid sweat, and javelina grease.

Fargo brought his rifle up too late. Screeching like a devil loosed from hell, the Indian dove off the boulder, a heavy-bladed knife glistening in his right fist, his left forearm smashing the Henry out of Fargo's grasp.

As the rifle clattered to the sand, Fargo flung his hands up, his right grabbing a handful of the Apache's hair as his left curled around the Indian's sinewy wrist, halting the razor-sharp blade's descent four inches from his left eye.

He wrestled the man's knife-wielding hand aside as the ground came up and struck his back.

Fargo grunted as the air left his lungs in a single blast, the Indian's savage screeching making his eardrums rattle. Dazed, Fargo maintained his hold on the Indian's wrist and his hair, stifling the man's attempts to raise the blade for another killing slash. The man's calico shirt was slick with blood, no doubt from Fargo's .44 round that had blown him off his horse.

As they wrestled, the Indian trying to slam his knees into Fargo's exposed groin, they rolled down a slight rise once, twice, three times. Fargo ground his own right knee into the Indian's groin.

"Ayeeee!" the Apache wailed, bathing Fargo's face in hot air and fetid spittle.

Fargo flung the man aside and leaped to his feet. The Indian gained his knees and began bolting toward Fargo. The Trailsman kicked the knife from the man's right hand. As the knife clattered into the brush, Fargo lunged forward, swinging his right foot up, smashing his curled toes under the man's chin.

The Indian grunted and flew ass over teakettle backward down the slope and out of sight.

Fargo wheeled, picked up his rifle, brushed the sand from the breech, and turned toward the dark slope where the Apache had disappeared.

Silence. Nothing moved amidst the gnarled, spindly shapes of the desert scrub.

Fargo moved slowly forward, breathing deeply to calm his racing heart, sweat and sand bathing him. Cat-stepping down the shelf, following the Indian's scuff marks in the sand, Fargo stopped before a low boulder, pricking his ears.

He'd begun lifting his gaze above the boulder when it sprang toward him suddenly, the Indian's keening wail sounding like the victory cries of a hundred plunging eagles.

Fargo spread his feet and, crouching, swung the Henry's barrel straight up and fired. The wail dropped several octaves as the Indian leaped straight up off his feet and, dropping the knife, flew backward five yards before smashing into a creosote shrub and hitting the ground in a silent heap.

The Trailsman jacked another shell into the Henry's

breech, the spent casing arcing over his right shoulder. He swabbed sweat from his brow with his left wrist, then moved slowly forward, keeping the Henry's barrel on the dark lump in the brush and gravel before him. He planted his right heel on the man's shoulder and heaved him over.

The man's calico bandanna had slid down over his left eye. The right was half open and blindly staring, lips parted in a gap-toothed death sneer. Fresh blood oozed from a hole in the top center of his chest.

Enervated voices rose from the other side of the wash to Fargo's left. He recognized the tones of the blacksmith-dentist, Haggelthorpe, and his two sons, growing louder as they moved his way.

Fargo cursed as he dropped his eyes to his sweat-soaked, sand-basted, naked body. He jogged back the way he'd come, but instead of heading into the wash, he traced the wash's western bank in the general direction of his camp, ducking under branches and leaping barrel cacti and creosote.

When he figured he was near his camp, he turned into the arroyo. He spent several minutes fumbling around in the dark before he nearly stumbled over Roy Dixon's body, slumped in the short grass, blood still oozing around the gaping hole in his back.

Fargo continued past the man to his near-dead fire and picked up his balbriggans lying twisted where he'd dropped them in his passion for Dixon's wife. "It's Fargo. Come on out." His voice betrayed his chagrin at having been caught with his pants not only down but *off*.

He shook out the long underwear and stepped into it. A slender figure materialized from the darkness. She was still clutching her dress to her bosom.

"Best get into that thing," Fargo said.

He buttoned up his balbriggans, then stirred the fire's dully glowing coals with a thin branch and tossed the branch on the coals. A flame leaped to life. Fargo

24

added more wood, the flame revealing the girl standing on the other side of the rock ring, regarding him fearfully.

"They gone?"

"For now."

Her thin voice trembled. "Who . . . ?"

"Bandits. Get dressed and follow me back to the main camp." He walked over to her and placed his hands on her shoulders. "You and your husband were out strolling when they hit. He took the hatchet in his back, and you hid in the brush. Got it?"

Her chest rose and fell sharply as she clutched the dress to her full breasts. "My God, Roy's dead."

She said it without feeling, almost as though she were running the idea through her head to see how she felt about it. Fargo thought that, other than fear for her own safety and maybe a little chagrin about what she'd been doing when Roy had taken the hatchet, her husband's demise was little more upsetting to Deana Dixon than, say, learning that her privy would soon need to be moved.

Fargo felt the same way. After all, that hatchet had probably saved his own life. . . .

He stared down at her. "Did you hear what I said?"

Her eyes rose to meet his and she nodded, then stepped away and shook out her dress.

When he and the girl were back in their clothes, she followed him contritely over to where her husband lay facedown in the grass, Dixon's hat tipped forward, the brim pinned beneath his forehead.

Fargo handed his rifle to Deana, then bent down, hoisted the man's limp body over his shoulder, and set his hat for the main camp. Deana trailed at a good distance, and, as Fargo made his way toward the low fire showing through the desert scrub, he hoped she'd arrange a properly heartbroken expression.

"It's Fargo!" he called when the wagons shone in the firelight ahead. "I'm comin' in!"

25

"Mr. Fargo!" cried Haggelthorpe's younger son, Peter, running over from his family's wagon, his bullet-crowned hat shading his eyes. "We was attacked by desperadoes or some such, and . . . " The boy's voice trailed off as his eyes slid to the body hanging over the Trailsman's shoulder.

Haggelthorpe and the other men—Jasper Felton, Owen Heinze, and Ben Leonard—moved up from the perimeter of the firelight, all looking harried and holding rifles. Haggelthorpe's older son, Jim, held an old Hawken rifle whose weathered stock was wrapped with shrunken rawhide. A bullet had burned a furrow across his right cheek.

His mother matched his steps as he walked with the other men toward Fargo. Mrs. Haggelthorpe clucked worriedly as she dabbed at the lanky younker's cut with a damp cloth.

The two other women in the group were sitting near the wagons, talking in hushed, enervated voices. Mrs. Felton was sobbing and showing Mrs. Heinz and Mrs. Leonard a bullet tear in her homespun dress sleeve. Fargo was glad to see everyone standing and accounted for.

"Ah . . . no. . . ." Merlin Haggelthorpe sighed, shaping a pained look when Fargo laid Roy Dixon's lifeless body down beside the fire. The Trailsman noted a lack of genuine feeling in the blacksmith-dentist's expression, however. No real remorse registered in the voices of the others, either. Dixon had been a pugnacious old cuss.

"This our only casualty?" Fargo asked.

Jasper Felton lifted his eyes from Dixon and ran a hand through his bib beard. "All of us here came through it without any major perforations, though Jim here came close. We heard gunfire across the wash. You give chase, Fargo?"

"I finished off one that you boys must've wounded. And I killed an Apache."

The dreaded word sent a ripple of fear through the

26

small crowd, Mrs. Haggelthorpe turning to Fargo sharply and gasping. Jim wrapped a hand around his mother as he turned to Fargo. "I seen him, too. The rest looked like Mexicans."

"The ones I seen were wearin' sombreros," said Ben Leonard, a short, middle-aged man with thinning, sandy hair and a full beard but no mustache.

"Well, there's—was, I should say—an Apache runnin' with 'em." Fargo stared off beyond the wagons. "How many did you see over here?"

"I counted four," Haggelthorpe said, turning a slow circle as he, too, scouted the area for more trouble. "With the Apache you killed, that'd make about five. We must've given more of a fight than they thought they could handle."

"Or," Mrs. Haggelthorpe said, turning an incriminating look on Deana Dixon, "maybe they didn't see what they were looking for over here . . ."

Deana stood near the Trailsman's right elbow, her eyes wide and frightened as she turned to the older, doughy-faced woman. "You mean . . . you think they were after . . . me?"

"Mabel," Haggelthorpe said, keeping his voice down. "There's no point in frightening the girl. She lost her husband this evening, for the love of God!"

Mabel Haggelthorpe slitted her eyes sarcastically as she shuttled her gaze between the girl and the tall Trailsman. "Oh, I'm quite certain *Mrs. Dixon* will make out just fine!"

With that, she wheeled and, hailing her two sons to follow her, stomped off toward the Haggelthorpe wagon.

"I'm sorry, Mrs. Dixon," Merlin Haggelthorpe said, doffing his hat and clutching it to his chest. "Mabel's just distraught. I'm sure she'll apologize her ownself in the mornin'."

The other men apologized for the girl's loss then, too, holding their hats and stepping up formally but not, Fargo saw, unable to let keep their eyes from roaming over Mrs. Dixon's exquisite frame. Deana thanked them for their ministrations, then, shuttling a furtive glance at Fargo on the other side of the fire, retired to her wagon.

Fargo caught himself watching her walk away. He turned to his right. The others were watching her, too. He cleared his throat, and they all jumped and donned their hats.

"Let's fan out," Fargo said. "Keep close watch on the camp. I doubt those hombres will be back tonight, but there's no point in taking chances."

Any *more* chances, he silently admonished himself.

"What about Dixon?" Owen Heinze asked, glancing down at the dead man.

"We'll bury him at first light, then get our asses on the trail for Genesis."

"What about Mrs. Dixon?" asked Jasper Felton, his voice thick as he stared at the girl's retreating ass swaying deliciously under her skirts.

"What's the matter, Felton?" Fargo asked. "One wife not enough for you?"

4

Fargo was an old hand at guiding pilgrims through trouble country; thus he was accustomed to going without sleep. He could go three or four days before the lack of rest began to bother him, and he could always make up for lost sleep with catnaps during the day, even while riding.

His current clients, however—none of whom slept much after the banditos' attack on their camp— appeared a mite peaked and grouchy the next morning as they stumbled around in the false dawn, whipping together a quick breakfast and burying Roy Dixon beneath a willow abutting a dry spring.

No one said much of anything aside from Jasper Felton, who, being a lay preacher and church deacon, offered a brief sermon and a few prayers over the grave, the last of which Fargo cut short with, "That's enough, Felton. If the Lord hasn't taken him by now, he's not going to."

Ignoring the haughty chuffs of the three older women, the Trailsman donned his hat, led Deana Dixon to her wagon, and lifted her into the driver's box. He climbed up beside her and untied the reins from the brake handle, glancing back at the others mounting their own rigs as the sun began blossoming behind the craggy eastern peaks, warming the cool night air.

"Keep the wagons tight together! If anyone needs to stop, call out loud and clear, and we'll all stop!"

"How much farther, Mr. Fargo?" Jasper Felton yelled from two wagons down the line as he wrestled his hefty wife onto his Conestoga.

"Barring more trouble, we should pull into Genesis in the early afternoon."

There was a murmur of relieved approval as Fargo kicked the brake free and shook the ribbons over Roy Dixon's two dun mules. The animals stepped into their collars, lowering their heads and pricking their ears, and the wagon squawked forward over small rocks and sage shrubs, angling southeast through a narrow cut between sandstone bluffs. Fargo's Ovaro, tied to the wagon's rear hitch, plodded along behind.

Deana Dixon rode silently to the Trailsman's right, hands in her lap, as they chewed up the dusty, sweaty miles, the sun rising before them like a giant lemon fire balloon. Fargo rode with his elbows on his knees, the ribbons loose in his hands.

He sensed that the girl was horrified by the attack but guiltily relieved that she no longer had Roy Dixon to order her around like a half-breed slave during the day, or to take his rough satisfaction at night.

"Skye?" she asked as they crossed a dry riverbed, scaring a flock of turkey buzzards up from a deer carcass.

His rangy body moving lazily with the wagon's jerk and sway, he glanced at her.

"When the others are settled in Genesis, will you take me back to Kansas?"

He stared at her, frowning. She looked around at the sunbaked clay and copper escarpments rising around them, and at the cholla, saguaros, and spindly mesquite lining ravines. "I don't like it here. Coming here was Roy's idea. He thought he'd get rich prospecting. I want to go back to Kansas City. I have a cousin there, and she'll take me in until I can figure out something on my own."

She closed her left hand around his forearm and gazed smokily into his eyes. "I don't have much money. Roy put most of it into mining supplies. But I'll make it worth your time . . . " She licked her lips and lowered her chin, smiling. Uncharacteristically, she wore her hair down, the thick, honey-blond mass framing her smooth-skinned face and sparkling eyes. She had also left the top two buttons of her shirtwaist undone, revealing just enough cleavage to tickle Fargo's memories of the night before—before her husband had so rudely sauntered into his camp, that was.

Fargo hadn't planned on backtracking, but he didn't have any other work lined up at the moment. Kansas was as good a place as any to find another wagon train in the market for a pilot. He glanced again at Deana's cleavage, then lifted his eyes to her face. "Since you're in mourning, Mrs. Dixon, I reckon it's only right that I offer any comfort that I can."

She looked away guiltily. He chuffed as he turned forward, trying to cover a real attachment he felt for the beauty, and put the mules up a low rise stippled with boulders and greasewood.

An hour after the group had nooned in a cottonwood grove along a trickling stream, the Trailsman spied the tracks of a dozen or so horses angling onto the trail before him.

They were all shod, so the riders weren't Indians. Maybe drovers or an Army detail, as the bluecoats were making more of a presence now that more settlers were filtering into the region, annoying the native Apaches. The only thing that troubled Fargo was that the horses had been moving at a fast clip—as though they were either chasing or being chased.

"What is it?" Deana asked, a worried note in her voice.

31

Tipping his head to the left, Fargo was scrutinizing the tracks and occasional horse apples littering the powdery dust and orange caliche.

He straightened and grunted, dismissing the question. No reason to upset her or the others. The horse-shit in the trail appeared two or three days old, so whomever had been through here was long gone . . . for now. . . .

Just the same, as the wagons continued churning the dry desert dust, Fargo kept his Henry close beside him and a sharp eye skinned on the low-lying areas and the ridge crests—anywhere an ambush might be effected. An hour after he'd spied the tracks, he drew back on the mules' reins, halting the wagon on the crest of a cedar-studded rise.

He stared down the grade into the wide, undulating valley before him. A green line of trees and grass followed a stream running along the base of burnt orange rimrock on the valley's other side.

"Why are we stopping?" Deana asked sleepily from the box behind Fargo, where she'd been napping.

The question was echoed by Jasper Felton running his wagon up to the Trailsman's left, and by Haggelthorpe on his right.

"I hope it's not trouble," said Felton, his sunburned, doughy-faced wife beside him staring warily into the valley below. "I sense we're close to our destination. To encounter more trouble now would be a cruel joke."

"You sensed correct, Felton." Fargo shifted around on the wagon's hard seat, throwing back his shoulders and stretching his spine. He stared straight ahead from under the brim of his high-crowned, broad-brimmed hat. "You're about two hundred yards from it."

"What do you mean, Fargo?" asked Merlin Haggelthorpe, holding his leather hat up to block the sunlight as he stared into the valley. "I see nothing but an empty valley, and Genesis is a sizable town!"

Haggelthorpe's wanly smiling wife, Mabel, and older son, Jim, sat beside him, while the youngster, Peter, poked his head out of the covered box behind them, eyes wide with expectance as he raked his gaze from left to right across the valley. Owen Heinze, flanked by Ben Leonard, drew his own wagon up on the other side of the Haggelthorpe rig and drew his dusty yellow neckerchief away from his nose, glancing at Fargo curiously.

"Your new home's just beyond that line of low bluffs yonder," Fargo said. He'd dug his makings sack from the pocket of his buckskin tunic and was building a cigarette. "I don't know how large you were told it was, but it nestles in that valley right nice."

"You don't say!" exclaimed Owen Heinze, his lower jaw falling and his eyes snapping wide. His wife squirmed around in her seat delightedly and grabbed her husband's right arm with both hands.

"Now hold on," Fargo said as he shaped the cigarette in his fingers.

But the warning was drowned by Heinze, who slapped his reins against his mules' sweat-silvered backs and shouted, "Well, what the hell we waiting for? We're home, fellers!"

"I said hold on!" Fargo shouted as all four other wagons bolted away from his, their iron-shod wheels churning red dust as they thundered down the valley's gentle ridge.

The men and boys were shouting gleefully, the mules braying, the women clapping their hands. They either hadn't heard the Trailsman's warning or, in their haste for the long trip to be over, were ignoring it.

Fargo scowled down the hill at the bouncing wagons and buffeting canvases, holding his half-rolled quirley in his thick fingers.

"What's the matter, Skye?" Deana asked.

With an angry chuff, Fargo glanced around at the

shod hoofprints marking the ridge—the same prints he'd spied earlier. They were barely noticeable, worn as they'd been by the wind, but the fast-moving riders had plainly been through here. Likely, they'd come and gone, but Fargo was still hearing vague warning bells tolling in his experience-tuned ears.

He tossed away the half-made quirley with a curse, then ordered Deana to hold on as he shook the ribbons over the mules' backs. Instantly, the wagon plunged down the side of the hill, the freight in the box shifting forward, the dust kicked up by the other four wagons stinging Fargo's eyes.

"I don't get it, Skye!" Deana said, glancing at him worriedly as she clutched her seat with both hands, the wagon's violent bouncing making her voice quiver. "What's wrong?"

"*Probably* nothing," Fargo said as he began closing the gap between him and the other wagons. Still, he saw no reason to go barreling into a town you hadn't scouted first. Frontier settlements weren't necessarily synonymous with safety, and Fargo always liked to scope them out before broiling down the main drag like a mustang with wolves on its heels.

Fargo stared straight ahead as the other four wagons, traveling abreast and about twenty feet apart, disappeared over the lip of the next ridge. He followed, gritting his teeth against the jarring, hoping the wagon didn't fall apart before he made the valley floor.

As it turned out, he didn't have to race that far. Cresting the second ridge and peering down the other side, he saw all four wagons lurching to skidding halts before him. Haggelthorpe's wagon had stopped so abruptly that the Trailsman had to jerk the mules sharply right to avoid a collision, cursing the blacksmith-dentist at the top of his lungs, then bounding to his feet to haul back on the reins with all his force.

He'd loosely wrapped the Ovaro's bridle reins to

the back hitch, in the event of just such a perilous maneuver. As the Dixon wagon ground to a halt, nearly throwing Deana forward over the dashboard, the pinto ran up on Fargo's left, regarding his master with the same exasperation with which Fargo now regarded the drivers of the four wagons now flanking him on either side.

"When I give a goddamn order—"

The Trailsman stopped when he saw the incredulous, horrified expression on Jasper Felton's bearded face as the man stared into the valley before them. Fargo followed his gaze. His stomach tightened instantly, and his eyes slitted. Unconsciously, his right hand slid to the grips of the big Colt jutting on his right hip.

"Oh, my God!" Deana Dixon whispered, slowly raising both hands to her mouth.

Fargo blinked, making sure that what he saw wasn't a mirage. But, no, it was the town, all right. Or what remained of it—the charred remnants lying in ruins were piled for a quarter mile along the bank of the stream. A couple of wood-framed and adobe-brick buildings remained, or half remained, scorched and gutted as they were, but most of the buildings were indistinguishable from each other.

Here and there thin streams of smoke curled from the rubble.

"I don't believe it," Merlin Haggelthorpe said on Fargo's right, his reins hanging slack in his hands. Tears were already beginning to trickle down his wife's cheeks. "The town's burned to the ground!"

The boys, Jim and Peter, turned to Fargo as if for an explanation.

Fargo handed the reins to Deana, then grabbed his Henry rifle and stepped off the wagon onto the saddle of the Ovaro, standing off the wagon's left front wheel. "Stay here," he ordered, jacking a round into the rifle's chamber one-handed. He reached forward, grabbed the drooping reins, then nudged the pinto's flanks with his heels.

As Fargo galloped the pinto down the hill, he didn't hear a peep out of the weary travelers behind him. When the pinto gained the valley floor, Fargo swung left and stared ahead as the ruined town grew before him, the first of the ash heaps closing on both sides of the well-worn trace.

The air still carried the fetor of charred lumber and flesh, though Fargo saw no human corpses. Bits of ash wisped in the breeze.

In several places, the town's main drag was clogged with rubble, and Fargo traced a twisting course amongst the jutting ruins. He noted the burned school and the bank and the half-charred, red-lettered sign of WRIGHT'S HARDWARE lying in the street near a pile of burned lumber and a dead horse that the scavengers had found. A small fire burned amongst the rubble of what Fargo took to have been the livery barn, given the scorched hay and the thick stench of burned horseflesh.

He continued past the gaping windows of a half-standing saloon, switching his gaze from left to right, occasionally brushing soot from his eyelashes. The Ovaro nickered anxiously and bunched its muscles beneath the saddle.

Fargo kept his voice calm as he held the Henry's brass butt plate snugly against his hip. "Easy, boy."

At the far end of town, near the black stone remains of the jailhouse, Fargo stopped and turned the horse back toward the ruins, swinging his gaze to the hills rising on both sides.

This wasn't the work of a wildfire. There wasn't enough scorched earth around the town. Might have been an accident, of course. In such hot, dry country it took only a carelessly discarded quirley or a knocked-over lamp to lay waste to this much town and more . . .

But Fargo didn't think the fire here had been an accident. He lifted his head and sniffed the breeze. Amidst the stenches of charred wood and bodies lay the distinctive smell of kerosene.

He remembered the tracks of the dozen fast-moving riders he'd spied earlier. About to swing the Ovaro in a broad circle around the town, he was knocked forward with a jolt, his left arm aching and burning as though he'd been clobbered with a miner's pick.

At the same time that his own blood splattered the Ovaro's neck, the boom of a heavy-caliber rifle echoed around the valley.

5

Fargo didn't so much dismount as let the pitching pinto unsaddle him.

Clutching the Henry in his right hand and feeling nausea from the lancing pain in his bloody left arm, he hit the ground on one foot. As another slug blew up dust and ash near the horse's thrashing front hooves, he let his own momentum carry him to the ground. He rolled off his right shoulder and dove behind a stock trough on the north side of the street.

As the Ovaro whinnied and galloped back through the ruined town, reins trailing and stirrups flapping like wings, the Trailsman swiped his hat from his head and edged a glance over the lip of the scorched trough.

The shots had come from the southeast. He raked his gaze along the brushy, rocky slopes beyond the cottonwoods and above the stream.

Smoke puffed from a nest of red boulders along a ridge crest about a hundred and fifty yards away, and Fargo ducked as the large-caliber round—from a Sharps or a Spencer, judging by the sound—hammered the trough, blowing up wood chunks and causing the entire trough to bounce against Fargo's right shoulder. The bark of the slug against the stout cottonwood planks made his ears ring.

"Skye!" a girl's voice yelled above the distant, wooden clatter of a wagon.

Fargo turned to peer right along the debris-littered

street. The Dixon wagon bounced along the trail at the other end of the town, Deana herself holding the reins, moving toward him as she swung the mules around the rubble. The other four wagons thundered behind her, one of the men yelling for Deana to stop.

"Stay there!" Fargo raised the Henry above the trough and triggered a shot at the boulders along the ridge crest.

The Henry wasn't accurate at that distance, but it might hold the bushwhacker's fire. Before his own shot had stopped echoing, Fargo had leaped up and over the trough and was sprinting toward the far side of the street.

He was in the open for about ten strides before, sensing another thimble-sized slug careening toward him, he dove toward the ash-flocked boardwalk fronting a couple of burned-out hulks.

He rolled up against the boardwalk as something slammed into a charred pillar above him with a *crunch* and a *twang*. As the thunder-like report sounded on the other side of the creek, Fargo looked up to see the remains of a porch roof, which had already been supported only by two spindly, charred pillars, shudder and lurch, then begin falling toward him.

Sucking air through his teeth as blood continued to dribble from his upper left arm—a flesh wound, he'd semiconsciously deemed the injury in spite of the throbbing pain—he sprang to both feet once more. He felt the swoosh of wind and heard the crunching thunder of the porch roof smashing onto the boardwalk behind him as he dashed forward along the street.

After six strides, he turned around a demolished coop fetid with the smell of scorched, rotting chickens, and traced a harried, zigzagging course through boulders and sage, angling toward the cottonwoods and the stream.

Another slug blew an arrow-shaped knob off a boulder to his right, and then he was in the cottonwoods.

He splashed into the stream as another shot boomed, but he was too close to the ridge base for the bushwhacker to plant a bead on him.

Trudging through the knee-deep water, he made the other side and ran east along the base of the ridge for fifty feet, then traced a gully lined with mesquite and creosote toward the crest. The shooting had stopped. The shooter was wondering where in the hell Fargo had gone, and he was no doubt getting worried, casting his gaze from left to right along the slope below his cover.

Fargo stopped to catch his wind beneath an overhanging rock. He glanced at his upper left arm. The buckskin tunic was blood-soaked, and he could feel more blood welling from the hole. Making use of the pause, he leaned the rifle against the rock, removed his red neckerchief, and retied it tightly over the bullet hole, sucking air through his teeth as the pain intensified.

That done, still gritting his teeth, his heart throbbing, he picked up the rifle and continued along the gully to the crest of the hill. He continued down the other side for fifty feet, crawled under mesquite and paloverde branches, then leaped to his feet. He jogged back up the back side of the rise. At the top, he aimed his rifle straight down the other side.

The nest of red rocks lay twenty feet before him, tufts of cactus and juniper pushing between the cracks. Nothing moved. Silence but for the rustle of the breeze and the incessant ring of a nearby cicada.

He tensed when something flashed in the air below and right of the rock nest. A cartridge casing arced high and then fell, clanked off a flat-topped boulder, and disappeared.

Fargo smiled coldly. The bushwhacker was trying to draw him out.

Holding the Henry out from his right hip in one hand, Fargo cat-footed down the rise. He stepped onto one of the boulders, moved left onto another rock, and hunkered down on his haunches, aiming the rifle into the shaded pocket below.

A big man crouched between the rocks, facing downslope. He wore a red plaid shirt, loose denim breeches, and a broad-brimmed black leather hat. A Sharps rifle was snugged to his left shoulder, but his head was lifted away from the stock, his face angling to the right, chin slightly dipped. Fargo could see his jaw move as he swallowed.

As the bushwhacker swatted absently at a fly with his gloved right hand, Fargo said quietly, "Hold it."

The bushwhacker tensed, his head lifting slightly, but he did not turn.

"Set the rifle down easy and shove it down the slope."

When the rifle lay several feet down the hill, Fargo said, "Turn around and raise your hands to your shoulders. Make any sudden movements, and I'll blow your tonsils out the back of your neck."

The man rolled onto his right shoulder. The head swung around until the broad, handsome face of a young, mustachioed black man—mid- to late twenties—faced Fargo, the obsidian eyes large, round, and bright with defiance and fear. The man's mahogany cheeks glistened with sweat, and a muscle in his jaw twitched. He wore suspenders, and his linsey-woolsey tunic was worn through in several places.

As the silence stretched, the fear in the black man's eyes dissolved, leaving only defiance. He bunched his brows. "If you're gonna kill me, kill me and get it over with, you son of a bitch!"

Fargo kept the rifle snugged up to his cheek. "Why were *you* trying to kill *me*?"

The young man opened his mouth to speak, but stopped. He squinted one eye and canted his head slightly to one side. "You . . . you're not him, are ya?"

"Not *who*?"

"El Oso Loco."

The Trailsman lowered the rifle but kept the barrel aimed at the man's belly. "Name's Fargo. Skye Fargo. I may not shave regular, but the last time I looked in a mirror, I didn't see any crazy bear. Who in the hell are *you*, and who in the hell is this El Oso Loco hombre?"

"I'm Jerry Squires." He jerked his head to indicate the burned town down the hill and across the stream behind him. "El Oso Loco is responsible for that."

Following the man's gaze, Fargo saw four wagons stopped on the trail west of town, a couple of the men holding rifles as they stood peering cautiously toward Fargo from behind their horses. The Dixon wagon was stopped behind a rubble pile, but Fargo couldn't see Deana.

Squires said, "Him and some crazy senorita and their gang of Mex cutthroats came through here and laid waste to the place three nights ago. Killed most everyone, includin' my pa. We ran the blacksmith shop. I buried who I could find. The last of them that survived—nine souls in all—left just this mornin', headin' back Texas-way."

He squinted the same eye again and jerked his head sideways. "Skye Fargo . . . The Trailsman?"

Fargo grunted, lowered the rifle, and hopscotched the rocks down to where Squires stood in his make-shift bunker. The Trailsman picked up the man's .52 Sharps and handed it to him. "Where'd you learn to shoot that cannon?"

"I hit ya?"

"Flesh wound."

"Sorry. I reckon I'm a might touchy."

"Under the circumstances, I'll overlook it."

"Pa and I hunted buff out on the Plains before he got gored, and we took up blacksmithin'. Came out here to fix miners' wagons." Squires lowered the Sharps to his side and turned his dark, pensive gaze down to the black heaps of the town, probably looking at the spot on which his and his father's shop had stood until three days ago. "Thirty-six of us put the town up in the better part of a year. Expected it to last a lot longer than this."

The Trailsman propped a boot on a rock and, resting his Henry's barrel on his right shoulder, again followed Squires's gaze across the stream. Deana Dixon stood on a rock between the town and the stream, peering up the scarp, shading her eyes with one hand. Fargo threw up his right arm to indicate he was all right.

"Why'd they do it?" Fargo asked.

Squires shrugged and gritted his teeth. "Meanness, mostly. I think they were all drunk. They robbed the bank, killed the town marshal who pulled double duty as the barber, and stole all the supplies from Duggans' mercantile. The fire started there. They used kerosene from the store to spread it while they whooped and hollered like demons. Pa was gut-shot. I dragged him down to our old mine yonder. By the time I got back to the town, it was an inferno."

"A girl rode with 'em?"

Squires nodded. " 'Senorita Diablo,' she's called. Her and El Oso Loco started raidin' these parts about six months ago, earned reputations amongst the prospectors and ranchers right fast. They'd never raided this far west . . . till three days ago."

"Have you notified the Army? I hear they're building a cantonment a ways north, to protect the Butterfield route."

"The soldiers they send out here ain't worth spit. 'Paches use 'em for torture practice." Squires plucked a braid of tobacco from his shirt pocket and raised it to Fargo, who shook his head. Squires bit off a plug and, returning the braid to his pocket, said, "I'm exacting my own pay . . . little by little."

Fargo frowned. "Pardon?"

Squires stared back at Fargo thoughtfully, then turned and leaped over a rock in the wall of his barricade, and tramped over the hill's northern shoulder. "Follow me."

Fargo stared after him skeptically, then jumped over the barricade wall and followed the young black man through the sage and greasewood until they'd traversed the hill's shoulder and were angling down the far side, toward a sheer wall of sandstone rising on the left. On the other side of the wall lay a broad gorge choked with ancient, dead cottonwoods stretching their bald, bleached limbs skyward.

Fargo tramped after Squires, moving into the forest abutted by the two-hundred-foot sandstone walls, and stopped. He stared straight ahead down the corridor of dead trees. Squires swung his head left and right as he walked, chin held proudly high.

Shadowed figures moved in the branches on either side of the black man. The figures were men hanging in the trees. Four men dressed in the traditional garb of the Mexican border bandit—short, leather jackets or serapes, bell-bottomed slacks, some decorated with hammered silver discs. Two wore cartridge belts crossed on their chests.

All four had been hanged. Their necks had been stretched a good four inches, hands tied behind their backs. Swollen tongues protruded from lips like ripe plumbs. Two of the bodies were bleached nearly as white as the branches they hung from, limbs stiffening, blood leaking from the eyes which buzzards and crows had been feeding upon.

Walking slowly forward, Fargo stopped and peered up at the last man, hanging from a stout limb on his right. The freshest one of the bunch—eyes pinched shut, curly salt-and-pepper hair fluttering in the hot breeze. A jagged pink scar hooked around his left, half-open eye. Fresh blood puddled on the man's shoulder, soaking his calico shirt and calfskin vest. He wore two empty holsters thonged low on his thighs.

"Stretched him just this morning," Squires said, holding the barrel of his Sharps across his right shoulder and staring proudly up at the scar-faced dead man.

Flies buzzed around the bodies—a steady hum nearly as loud as the cicadas. The death stench was almost palpable. Oily fingers clawing at the back of Fargo's throat, he fought back a retch and said, with one eye narrowed at Squires, "The raiding party, I take it?"

"They done split up, and I done tracked five to a gulch about six miles south of here. Ambushed 'em while they was drunk on corn whiskey. Killed one outright. I hanged these others real slow, one at a time." Squires's voice hardened. "Hanged 'em so's the others could hear their squeals as they died. Then I hanged the last one while the son of a bitch beside him was still alive to watch."

He turned to Fargo. "I figured for sure you was El Oso Loco come lookin' for his *compañeros*. Why don't you let me tend that arm for you? You're lookin' a might peaked."

Fargo wasn't surprised that he looked peaked, and he didn't think it was only the wound making him look that way. He'd seen men hanged before, but it wasn't an image a man got accustomed to.

The Trailsman raked his gaze away from the dead man's purple tongue and regarded Squires skeptically. "You intend on tracking the rest of the gang, do you?"

Squires hiked a shoulder. "I'll look for 'em, but they're probably in Mexico by now. There's Rurales down there, and they're *muy* bad hombres to mess with. I couldn't do it alone." He cast Fargo a speculative glance. "Say, you wouldn't wanna throw in with me, would ya?"

Fargo shook his head. "I'm sorry about what happened to your people, but I gotta help this wagon train figure out what they're gonna do, and where they're gonna go." He turned and began tramping back the way he'd come, between the grisly hanging corpses squawking their ropes and baking in the desert sun. "Hell of a damn pickle," he muttered.

"You can camp with me down by the creek," Squires called behind him. "Plenty of fresh water and graze, and I got some jerked deer meat, too!"

The Trailsman threw up an arm in acknowledgment, then started up the hill, weaving around sunbaked rocks and cacti. He was halfway to the top when the Ovaro appeared suddenly at the crest of the hill, looking down at him and tossing his head.

Fargo scowled up at the horse. "Where the hell have you been?"

Cresting the rise, he grabbed the horse's reins, toed a stirrup, and hauled himself into the leather. He trotted the stallion down the hill's other side and stopped beside Deana Dixon, who was kneeling near a spring and cupping water to her face. The water had run down into her shirt, and the wet muslin would have been a nice effect had Fargo not just come upon a burned town, hanging corpses, and a revenge-hungry man who'd drilled a thimble-sized hunk of lead through his arm.

He dismounted beside Deana, who sat back on her heels, staring at the charred remains of the town in shock while wisps of damp hair danced about her face.

"What the hell are you doing out here alone?" Fargo asked, hitching his pants up at the thighs and kneeling to cup water to his stinging upper arm.

"I was following you." She turned to him, frowning. "You're not an easy man to keep up with."

"You shouldn't try."

She glanced at his bloody arm. "Who's going to tend your wounds?"

46

He'd gently removed the neckerchief from his wounded arm, and she grabbed it out of his hands. She soaked it in the springwater and wrapped it tautly around the wound. "Doesn't look too bad," she said like a mother tending an accident-prone child. "That should hold until we can set up camp and I can boil some water."

"I got more important matters to tend to now."

He stood and crawled back into the leather, then stretched his hand to her. She took it, and he hauled her up behind him.

"A whole town burned," Deana Dixon said behind him. "What happened, Skye? What's going to happen to us?"

Fargo galloped the Ovaro back toward the charred humps of Genesis. "Good questions."

6

Fargo booted the Ovaro back through the rubble of the ruined town. Reaching the Dixon wagon, he handed Deana into the driver's box before riding back to the wagon's rear.

He held the pinto's reins in one hand as he slid out of the saddle and into the wagon's freight box, then quickly looped the reins over an eye hasp on the tailgate. He negotiated his way through the Dixons' cluttered cargo, then shoved through the cover's front pucker and sat down in the driver's seat beside Deana.

"Next time I give you an order," he said as he unwrapped the reins from the brake handle, "follow it. You could have ridden into an ambush."

She gave him a hurt look and angrily flicked a lock of honey-blond hair from her face. "I was worried about you."

"Don't worry about me. Just listen to me."

He flicked the reins, found a wide spot in the street between humps of charred debris, and turned the wagon around. The other four wagons waited fifty yards beyond, the settlers standing around staring in awe at the town they'd intended to call home but which was now only a heap of ashes in Bone Creek Canyon.

When Fargo pulled even with Haggelthorpe's team, the men, women, and two youngsters stared up at him dumbly, as if their tongues had been cut out. All except Merlin Haggelthorpe, who mopped sweat from his left cheek with his wrist and said, "Apaches?"

"Banditos. Burned the town three days ago after a bank robbery. Those who survived, and there weren't many, lit a shuck."

"You think the bandits were part of the same band that attacked us last night?"

"I wouldn't bet against it."

Jasper Felton turned away from the town while his wife, crying silently, continued staring at the heaps of ash and half-burned timbers from which rock foundations and chimneys and occasional wagon wheels protruded. Felton's voice sounded dull and far away. "What was the shooting about, Fargo?"

"One of the survivors took me for a bandit. We'll head downstream a mile or so, make camp, and talk about what you want to do next. We'd best not dally here."

Murmurs of agreement rose.

Fargo shook the ribbons across the mules' backs and headed west along the valley. He held the mules to a slow walk until the other wagons had turned around and caught up to him, and then he stepped the team up, following a wagon trail—one gouged by ore wagons from the area's mines, no doubt—paralleling the stream.

Prospectors and miners would probably remain in the valley, as they were a hardy lot who could hide from trouble in the desert mountains and rimrocks, but it was no longer a place for townsfolk. It wouldn't be until the Army and the law could establish a toehold against outlawry, which wasn't likely to happen while they were preoccupied with the Apaches. . . .

Fargo put the wagon across the stream and directed the settlers to bivouac along a caliche flat under a broad obelisk jutting out from the rimrock above. He unhitched Deana's team, then fed and watered the animals, rubbed them down, and tended their hooves before picketing them with the other mules in deep grass in a nearby cottonwood grove.

He'd mounted the Ovaro and begun riding upstream, climbing the creosote-stippled slope toward the caprock when he spied a lean-to fashioned from an old Army tent wedged against another overhang about seventy yards away.

The canvas ruffled in the wind, as did the tail of the horse picketed near a stone fire ring.

Squires's camp.

The Trailsman winced. He understood the young man's desire for revenge, but hanging the banditos so close to where he camped was an unnecessary danger. Fargo would have liked to move the settlers even farther away from the hanging boneyard, but the mules were tuckered as it was, and so were the pilgrims. They'd move out first thing in the morning and find another place to camp, a couple of miles away, while they rested the animals, made repairs to the wagons, and refigured their plans.

Fargo found a narrow crevice in the sandstone rocks up the grade from the settlers' bivouac—a sheltered place with a broad view of the open ground across the cottonwoods and the creek. He tended the pinto, taking extra time with the fine-boned stallion's coat and hooves, then turned it loose to forage in a nearby, spring-fed box canyon where the grama grass grew lush amongst willows, paloverde, and Mormon tea. He built a low fire at the mouth of the box canyon and made coffee.

Taking his coffee cup in one hand, the rifle in the other, he mounted the knoll on the north side of his camp and sat on a flat rock near a stunted piñon, sipping the coffee and watching the settlers rustling amongst the wagons below and to his left.

He was glad to be off by himself. He could see, hear, and think better alone.

The Trailsman had realized long ago, when just a

boy—and this was one of the main reasons he'd come west in the first place—that he was more alone with people than he ever was by himself, with a sage-carpeted desert spread around him, or snow-flocked mountains looming over him. Alone, there was nothing to compromise his inborn clarity.

He needed that clarity as much as he'd ever needed it, if he was going to keep the pilgrims out of the hands of bandits or Apaches. But for some reason, when he'd filled his canteens at the creek and taken a quick look around, noting Jerry Squires moving about the lean-to on the knoll, he didn't regret seeing Deana Dixon strolling up the grade from the settlers' bivouac.

She moved with the comely grace of the high-bred, her long skirts caressing her long, fine legs, her full bust jouncing behind a tight, low-cut shirtwaist as she climbed the hill. She'd combed out her hair and secured it in a French braid behind her head. In one hand, she carried a jackrabbit by its back legs, the rabbit's head bouncing off her leg as she walked.

Gaining the crest of the ridge, where Fargo sat on the flat rock, his coffee cup in his hands, a whiskey bottle resting beside his bent knee, she held the rabbit high and smiled. "Snared him myself. The Skye Fargo method you taught me. A broad loop, smooth slipknot rubbed in nut butter, and a watchful eye."

He stared up at her, ran his baldly appraising gaze down her high, clean-lined cheeks to her neck and upthrust bosom, the deep cleavage revealed by the shirtwaist. He didn't mind a comely woman in his camp. Never had. Just as long as she didn't get proprietary—a problem with the well-blooded breeds, he'd noted. This one would get the message eventually.

Until then . . .

He looked at the jack. "I'll be damned. You snared that yourself?"

"I'm more self-sufficient than either you or my husband thought. Shall I roast him for you?"

"The other women run you out of camp?"

"I get the impression they don't want me around their men."

The Trailsman ran his eyes up and down her again, noting her saucily jutted hip. "No wonder."

"I'll go roast him." She moved off down the rise toward his fire, and he glanced over his shoulder at the sway of her firm butt behind the skirt, reminding himself to not get caught with his pants literally down again, as he had last night.

While Deana roasted the rabbit, Fargo gathered wild roots and desert vegetables to add to their meal. She made him sit long enough for her to clean and bandage the wound in his left arm. When the rabbit had turned a deep, golden brown, the skin cracking and juices sizzling in the glowing coals, they sat around the fire as the falling sun turned the western sky into a painter's pallet of reds and yellows, and washed the meat and raw vegetables down with coffee laced with whiskey.

After supper, he and Deana walked down the hill to the settlers' camp, where the women gave Deana incriminating looks. Deana retreated to her wagon while Fargo and the other men, including Haggelthorpe's two boys, discussed the situation around the fire, upon which a kettle of soup bubbled. The blacksmith-dentist announced that he'd like to try his luck at the fledgling gold camp called Tombstone about fifty miles northeast in the Dragoon Range. Since the others had no other ideas, they decided to follow Haggelthorpe's lead.

The Trailsman agreed to lead them there before taking Deana back to Kansas, but first they'd move their camp to another valley a good distance from the grisly cottonwood grove, give the mule teams time to rest and replenish themselves on good grass and water, and allow the men and women time to repair cracked axles, bent wheel rims, torn canvas, and other sundry mendings part and parcel to any overland wagon journey, as well as time to repack their cargoes.

Not long after they'd finished discussing their plans, Jerry Squires came over from his bivouac with a sack of dried venison and a deer heart wrapped in burlap. The women, including Deana, stepped up to the fire to be introduced to their shy Negro visitor, who shook hands with the men, nodded to the women, and accepted a cup of coffee from Mrs. Leonard to which Fargo added a splash of whiskey.

Obviously shy around strangers, Squires hadn't been sitting around the fire long, answering the men's questions about the raid on Genesis, before he stood, tossed his coffee grounds on the fire, hitched up his pants, and ran his wrist over his mouth in agitation.

"Best be getting back to my lean-to." He cast a dark, meaningful glance at Fargo. "I'm gonna hit the trail again early."

"Goin' after another one?" Fargo squinted over the rim of his coffee cup.

"That's right."

"They're probably all in Mexico by now, Squires." At least, Fargo hoped they were, and not backtracking Squires to what remained of Genesis. "You'd best give up the hunt; start thinking about the future."

"With all due respect, Mr. Fargo, you didn't watch those varmints kill your pa and burn your town around you. I reckon I'll find out if they're in Mexico or not . . . or just where they are. . . ."

Squires ticked his hat brim to the men, bid adieu to the women busily toiling in the shadows around the parked wagons, one fetching water from the creek. The black man started away, stopped, and turned back toward the fire. "There's a nice valley over the second ridge west, with grass, water, and plenty of cover. Good place to drive your picket pins for a few days."

Fargo and the pilgrims thanked Squires for the tip, then sat in pensive silence as they watched him drift off into the shadows beyond the fire. No one said anything before Fargo finished his coffee, picked up his rifle, and rose from his rock.

"Two-hour watches all night." He cast his gaze about the six male faces aglow in the guttering firelight. "I'll let you decide which shifts you take. Keep the fire low. I'll be around all night."

With that, he turned and tramped off into the darkness, heading upstream to scout around, cutting north across the creek and then swinging back downstream, following the creek until the charred humps of Genesis showed in the darkness. Judging by the snarls and yips, coyotes were fighting over scavenged carcasses.

An hour later, Fargo tramped back up the hill to his camp, slowing when he saw his fire had been built up, the dancing flames reflecting off the crenellated sandstone walls and tough brown grass jutting from their bases. He raised his Henry as he approached the mouth of the box canyon, then stopped at the edge of the firelight.

Deana Dixon lay curled in his bedroll on the right side of the fire, his blankets drawn up to her chin, her gold-blond hair fanned across his saddle. One bare shoulder and a naked knee protruded from the blankets. Her eyes were lightly closed, and the blankets rose and fell deeply as she breathed, dead asleep.

Fargo scowled down at her. Damn her to tempt him like this . . . again. She'd be safer in her wagon, for he intended to keep watch on the valley from the ridge above, but she looked so peaceful that he didn't have the heart to roust her.

She'd made fresh coffee before going to sleep, the pot chugging softly on a flat rock at the edge of the fire ring. His charred, dented cup sat nearby, waiting for him.

He glanced at her as he knelt on one knee and filled the cup. Beautiful and handy. Hard to beat a combination like that. He just hoped he could get her back to Kansas in one piece.

When he'd finished the coffee, Fargo checked on the pinto standing contentedly in the box canyon, enjoying the rest and the cool desert evening, then climbed the canyon's back wall to the rocky ridge crest. When he'd caught his breath, he strode back and forth along the undulating caprock, watching over the dark valley dropping below where, two hundred feet away, the pilgrims' fire flickered like a small, distant torch. Beyond, the creek shone like a silver-scaled, black snake between the rustling cottonwoods.

To the south, the escarpment—covered with a thin layer of sandy soil and gravel, and pocked with bunch-grass and cacti—shelved away into darkness.

Fargo was squatting on his haunches directly above the pilgrims' camp, rolling a cigarette, when a sound rose from behind him. He dropped the makings and lifted the Henry from across his thighs, gently levering a fresh round into the chamber, and straightening.

The sound came again—a heavy foot stepping down in dry brush. Fargo sniffed the air—he'd developed a keen sense of smell and could detect a man or horse within forty yards—but there was no breeze, and his nostrils picked up little but dry earth, sage, and juniper, with a tinge of pine from the higher elevations.

Wedging the Henry's butt against his hip and holding the barrel up at a slant, he moved southward down the shelving caprock. Twenty yards down the exposed bedrock of the ridge crest, the sage and cacti began, with juniper shrubs and scattered rocks here and there. He continued down the shelf, the night closing around him, hearing the sound of crunching brush twice more.

A black gap appeared before him. A ravine. He was

ten feet from the lip when the sound of a falling stone reached his ears, followed by the *clack* as it struck bottom.

Fargo paused, listening and holding the rifle in both hands, then crept forward and hunkered down on his haunches as he stared over the lip of the ridge and into the ravine yawning before him. An old watercourse, it appeared—forty yards wide at its widest, and winding between jagged, rocky walls. From below came the mineral smell of damp rock and verdant brush.

He couldn't see much, but there must be a spring or freshet at the bottom.

The thought was clipped by a sudden, hair-raising snarl. Fargo jerked his head up slightly and stared nearly straight out across the gap. Two eyes glowed at him from the darkness, and the cat's shape composed itself against the black velvet wall of the opposite ridge, about ten feet down from the lip. The mountain lion's tail swished back and forth stiffly, and an angry whine rose from deep in its throat.

Tensing, Fargo squeezed the rifle in his hands and stared at the two eyes showing in the middle of the lion's heart-shaped head, its ears laid partially back against its skull.

"Sorry, friend," the Trailsman said, keeping his voice low, dragging out the words with forced calm. "You go your way; I'll go mine."

He had no wish to shoot the cat. He never shot anything unless he was hungry or protecting himself. Some men shot animals as a matter of course or for sport. To Fargo's mind, sport killing was for red-eyed losers and tinhorns. Every animal had as much right to life as any human—more so than some humans Fargo had known.

The Trailsman had no quarrel with the cat . . . as long as the cat had no quarrel with him. Knowing, however, that the beast could bound across the gap in seconds and tear him limb from limb, he kept his finger on the Henry's trigger, prepared to aim.

Stretched seconds passed, Fargo breathing shallowly, gripping the rifle tightly.

Finally, the cat lifted its head and snarled again, the grating sound lifting the hair on the back of the Trailsman's neck. The cat flicked its tail before bounding up the opposite wall, slithering over the lip of the ridge, and disappearing into the southern darkness.

Fargo loosed a long, held breath and lowered the rifle's barrel.

He tensed again suddenly, jerking his head up.

Back in the direction of the pilgrims' camp, guns popped and horses thundered.

A woman screamed.

7

Sprinting back the way he'd come, Fargo was halfway to the lip of the ridge when the shooting rose in earnest, sounding like a small war in the valley below. Hooves thundered. Men shouted. Women screamed. One of the Haggelthorpe boys' yells was muffled with distance and nearly drowned by the gunfire.

"Pa . . . *help* . . . !"

Fargo ran up the grade, digging his heels into the ridge, pumping his arms. His gut soured when, peering straight out over the caprock, he saw a burnt-orange glow that brightened steadily, as though a giant lamp wick were being turned up.

The Trailsman hunkered down at the lip of the ridge and stared into the valley, seeing little but scurrying shadows and the glow of the burning wagons down along the creek. There were the intermittent pops of pistols and rifles, and the mules were screaming, but he was too far away to draw a bead on a marauder without risking hitting one of the pilgrims.

Cursing, Fargo clambered back to his feet and ran east along the rimrock angling down toward the box canyon and his own encampment. In the darkness, his boot clipped a stone. He fell and rolled, but managed to hang on to the Henry. Getting his feet beneath him, he continued running, boots grinding gravel and clacking on the uneven bedrock. To help the pilgrims, he had to get down to the valley floor, where he'd have a clear shot at their attackers.

As he moved east along the lip of the rim, the pops and booms of the gunfire, the thunder of the rampaging riders, and the screams of the women and mules grew louder.

He reached the notch through which he'd climbed up out of the box canyon. He set the Henry on the ground, dropped his legs over the shelf, then, planting his boots on two rocks below, turned and grabbed the Henry. Starting down the steeply pitched grade through the broken granite and sandstone and tufts of cacti, he clutched the Henry in his right hand while using his left to break his descent.

Twenty feet from the bottom, he realized the gunfire had died. Aside from his own labored breaths and the scuffs and clomps of his boots on the rock, the declivity through which he descended toward the canyon floor had fallen silent as a crypt.

He squeezed through a funnel and planted his right boot between two boulders. A scream rose from the mouth of the box canyon.

"Skyyyye! Help!" A stretched pause. Then, desperately: *"Nooooooo!"*

Deana.

Fargo dropped his left boot quickly and put too much weight on it without testing it first. The rock beneath the heel gave. His leg jerked straight down. Fargo released the rifle to flail for a hold on the right side of the chute, but the tips of his fingers only grazed the rock wall before he plummeted straight down the notch.

Talus rock followed him down, bouncing off the walls and washing over and under him. He bounced over a bulge in the bedrock, and rolled until the wall gave way to air.

The canyon floor thrust up from below with merciless speed and solidity.

"Uhffff!" Fargo grunted as the air was pounded from his lungs.

Something hard-edged smashed his right temple, setting up an off-key, pianolike clattering in his brain. He tried to lift his head but it weighed a boulder. His eyes grew heavy. Stone rained on him, tumbling out of the notch like coal from a chute.

His lids closed down, and his body went limp as a wet rag.

He only vaguely heard Deana Dixon's brittle, muffled voice scream once more and call his name, before a shouted Spanish curse and the smack of a fist silenced it.

The young Mexican woman known as Senorita Diablo sat her white Spanish barb near the burning wagons, feeling satisfied. She raised a long, black cigarillo to her lips.

Her raid on the gringos' encampment was all but over, and she was waiting for her gang to finish looting the pilgrims' belongings, including their livestock, and regroup.

She plucked a lucifer from the pocket of her deerskin vest, which was all that covered her full, sweat-glistening bosom. Shuttling her lustrous brown eyes around the bodies of the dead pilgrims crumpled and bleeding before her, and glancing at her own two men fixing halters and lead ropes to the mules they'd discovered in the cottonwoods, she scratched the lucifer to life on a silver concho trimming the barb's tooled-leather bridle straps.

A groan sounded on her left. Holding the match to the cigar, she calmly reached across her waist with her right hand, plucked one of the two matched Allen and Wheelock .32 revolvers from its cross-draw holster, and thumbed back the hammer. She tossed down the lucifer and turned to see a scrawny man with a gray bib beard rise up on his knees, blood running down his face and trickling from several bullet holes in his chest and arms.

His chin lifted and his mouth opened wide, as though he were about to beseech the Almighty. Senorita Diablo extended the revolver at him and fired, rendering the scream stillborn and punching the man's body back flat against the legs of a prostrate woman whose dress smoldered with cinders from the burning wagons.

The man threw his arms straight out, and his entire body twitched before gradually growing still.

Beyond the burning wagons, horses splashed in the stream—four or five mounts moving fast, hooves clattering on the rocks. Senorita Diablo holstered her revolver and sat her saddle, dragging on the cigarillo and blowing smoke out through her nostrils until three sombrero-clad riders approached from the left side of the burning wagons, their guns and knives flashing in the fire- and starlight. Two more approached from the right.

The two men on the right swung toward the senorita, both dragging something at the ends of their ropes. The lead rider, a hawklike ex-Rurale named Juan Guardia, checked his mustang down and said in Spanish, "We come bearing gifts, Senorita!"

He slid out of his saddle and, batwing chaps winging about his bell-bottom trousers, strode over to the blond-headed bundle lying facedown on the caliche behind Garcia's horse. He squatted down and lifted the head by the hair, tilting the young man's face toward the senorita. She inspected it coolly.

The boy's eyelids fluttered, lips stretching back from his teeth, blood streaking his cheeks. He appeared about fourteen or fifteen.

"If you haven't killed him, fool, we'll take him back to the miners," said Senorita Diablo, blowing a long smoke plume. "Is the other alive?"

"*Sí, Senorita,*" said the other rider, who'd dismounted and was prodding the other youngster's side with his boot. The young man—two or three years older than the first—rose to his hands and knees, convulsing as he vomited creek water. "Strong, too. He fought the rope well before I laid him out with my pistol butt. He will work long hours!"

"Tie them both to mules."

The two riders tied the boys' hands behind their backs and threw them over their horses. The younger boy sobbed and called for his father while the older youth went along in stoic silence, grunting and holding his side, occasionally coughing up more creek water. The two bandits hauled them off toward the mules, which the other bandits were gathering in the cottonwoods.

"Senorita . . . El Oso Loco!" A bulky bandito from Juarez extended his stubby brown finger. Three more silhouetted riders approached from the grade rising south of the creek. The moon was up, illuminating high, gauzy clouds. The riders' dust rose like smoke around the sage, rocks, and junipers.

"Where the hell has he been?" the woman muttered with customary petulance. "Suppose we'd run into *soldados* out here. Some help he'd have been!"

She spurred the barb toward the oncoming riders, angling up the low rise. The cream barb lunged off its rear hooves, neck arched regally.

"Did you get lost?" she yelled as she drew abreast of the lead rider—a tall, broad-shouldered hombre in a striped serape and buckskin pants tucked into his mule-eared boots. He wore two pistols on his hips—a pepperbox revolver and a big Colt Dragoon—and a Sharps rifle hung down his back by a leather lanyard. He had one milky eye, the result of a Yaqui saber blow, and it glowed in the darkness as if lit from behind.

The big man sighed and glanced at the man beside him. "She asks if we were lost, Manuelo." He turned to the girl, his smile tensing. "You go after fat pilgrims relaxing around fires, and we take the sharpshooter in the rocks, and you ask what took us so long . . ."

The senorita's barb turned a complete circle and lifted its nose high, giving an enervated whinny. She drew back on the reins and frowned at the big man—El Oso Loco was well over six and a half feet tall—sitting atop his clean-lined, broad-chested Appaloosa. "What sharpshooter? What are you talking about, liar? You've just become soft in your old age, *mi amor!*"

The big man laughed, his good eye slitting as it flicked to the girl's angrily heaving bosom while the other continued to glow. "It's true. He started shooting at us from the brush along the creek." El Oso Loco stretched to look up the rise, where a white canvas lean-to fluttered in the moonlight. "You didn't hear because you and the others were screaming like banshees as you attacked the main camp. How many times have I told you that when raiding a camp, keep your lovely mouth *shut . . . mi amor?*"

Senorita Diablo lifted her head sharply. Her thick, black hair fell down behind her bare shoulders, full breasts jutting behind the sweat-damp deerskin vest, which revealed a good half of her deep cleavage. She stuck the cigar between her lips and drew the smoke deep into her lungs with an insolent air, then blew it out quickly through flared nostrils. "Your mother was a goat, and you smell bad enough to choke a dog off a gut wagon. I scream when I attack because it makes me feel like the cold-hearted whore of the devil himself. Now, answer my question, or I will cut off your *cojones* and wear them for a necklace!"

El Oso Loco laughed. "You are the only woman in the world who can talk to me like that and keep her tongue, *chiquita.*"

He jerked his head toward the rear of his horse, where a taut rope angled sharply back from his saddle horn to the brush behind him. Fifteen feet behind the Appaloosa, a dark figure lay between two rocks, partially concealed by junipers.

Senorita Diablo spurred the barb toward the figure and dropped from her saddle, hitting the ground flat-footed. She knelt in the brush where the man lay face-down, the rope tying both wrists together and stretching his arms in front of his head. His breath rattled. He groaned almost inaudibly. Senorita Diablo lifted his head by his short, tightly curled hair, and peered into his hideously swollen face.

"Un hombre negro?" the girl said, looking up at El Oso Loco. "This is your *tirador de primera*?"

"He had a very large rifle!" exclaimed the rider sitting a steeldust gelding directly behind El Oso Loco's Appaloosa.

El Oso Loco was hipped around in his saddle. "His horse's shoes bore the markings we tracked to our *compañeros* hanging in the cottonwoods."

Senorita Diablo looked down at the injured man, slitting her eyes and bunching her lips with fury. "Ah . . . *sí.*"

"I thought you might want to finish him. It is my gift to you, *mi amor.*"

She released the man's head, which dropped in the brush with a thud, and rose stiffly. Her voice was taut with checked-down rage. "We will drag him till there is nothing left but bones, and then we leave his bones to the *zopilotes*!"

A woman groaned nearby. The senorita wheeled to see the third rider's mount, partially concealed by a cottonwood, skitter-step with a start. Holding his reins taut in his left hand, the man slammed his right fist down toward his saddle horn. There was a shrill grunt, and the figure draped across the horse's withers thrashed feebly, sobbing.

"No . . . please . . ."

Senorita Diablo studied the long shadow hanging

by the rider's left stirrup, tangled blond hair nearly brushing the ground. She smiled icily at El Oso Loco. "And what other prizes did you find, *mi amor*?"

"A nice reward for the men."

The senorita sneered at her lover. "For the *men*, huh?"

She strolled, rolling her hips insouciantly, to the horse of the third rider, Alberto Dominguez, whose crossed bandoliers glistened in the starlight. The mestizo smelled like wet leather and javelina. He shuttled his deep-set eyes guardedly between Senorita Diablo and the girl sprawled across the horse before him, placing a proprietary hand on the girl's ass, like an overgrown child afraid his toy is about to be taken away.

The senorita lifted the prisoner's head by a fistful of blond hair, kneeling down to stare at her face. The woman winced at the pain, tears streaking her dusty cheeks. Her cracked lip did little to mar her beauty.

Senorita Diablo glanced at El Oso Loco, one brow arched. "Nice find, *mi amor*."

She reached up, grabbed the woman around the waist, and jerked her off the horse. Dominguez frowned down at his female leader, grunting a protest, his right hand falling impulsively upon the grips of the .44 in his shoulder holster. The big man must have valued his life, however, for he left the revolver sheathed.

The blonde hit the ground awkwardly, with a groan, her hands tied behind her back. She rolled in the brush, legs thrashing. Senorita Diablo grabbed her arm and jerked her up to her knees. The gringa hung her head, shoulders jerking as she sobbed. "Please . . . I didn't do anything to you. . . ."

Senorita Diablo dropped to one knee before the pretty *norteamericana*, who wore a torn skirt and a thin chemise, and brushed the gold-blond hair back from her face. She took the girl's chin in her right hand, turned it this way and that as she inspected her clean-lined, wide-mouthed, aristocratic features. The girl stared back at her, eyes bright with fear, blood trickling from the right corner of her bottom lip.

Senorita Diablo dropped her hand to the girl's chemise and ripped it down the middle. The breasts hung bare—pale and full, with a small birthmark just below the pink right nipple. The gringa's waist was narrow, the hips flaring nicely, her belly heaving in and out as she breathed. Her eyes flashed rage as she glared at Senorita Diablo, her jaws set tight.

Above the women, Alberto Dominquez groaned like a love-hungry dog.

Senorita Diablo cupped the gringa's left breast in her right hand and offered a taunting smile. "Niiice . . ."

The girl spat in the senorita's face. She paid for it with a hard slap that threw her sideways to the ground. Senorita Diablo laughed, wiped her cheek with her arm, and turned to El Oso Loco. "She'll bring in some nice lucre when we sell her to the *federales* in Sonora. I don't want her ruined . . . any more than she already has been." She turned a sharp eye to Dominguez, who was staring at her with ridged brows and bunched lips. "*Comprende*, Senor Dominquez?"

The big, ugly half-breed with the Volcanic Arms repeater hanging down his back scrubbed his gray-bristled cheek with a gloved hand. The fingers of the glove had been hacked off for an easier grip on his weapon. He turned to El Oso Loco for help.

The latter grinned and shrugged.

The mestizo turned away. *"Sí, Senorita."*

"Throw her over my horse," Senorita Diablo ordered. "I'll watch her myself."

Muttering angrily in his customary hodgepodge of Spanish and Indian, not meeting the senorita's haughty gaze, Dominguez crawled down off his horse with a great cracking of oiled leather. He scooped up the blonde as if she weighed no more than a sack of grain, and set her roughly on the senorita's horse. He raked his hungry eyes across the sobbing blonde's exposed breasts, then turned and ambled to his own steeldust, and swung into the hurricane deck.

"Come on, pigs!" the senorita shouted at the other banditos, still milling about the pilgrims' ruined camp and burning wagons, several sifting through trunks for valuables. "What are you doing over there—playing with each other? *Vamonos!*"

With that, Senorita Diablo swung into the saddle in front of the slumped blonde and booted the white barb upstream toward the ruined town.

El Oso Loco tipped his hat back and stared after her, chuckling, his milky eye glowing as it caught the moonlight directly. As the horses of the other bandits thundered toward him, he glanced at Reyes and the dour-looking Dominguez, and spurred his own mount into a gallop after the women.

"You heard the senorita!"

Behind El Oso Loco's stallion, the body of the half-dead black man jerked along at the end of the rope, twisting, rolling, and caroming off boulders.

The man's miserable grunts and groans were buried beneath the rataplan of the horses' hooves.

8

A brush swept across the top of the Trailsman's head.

Sleep gripped him hard, however. That was all right. He didn't want to awaken, because he knew that somewhere up where consciousness lay, also lay excruciating pain—hot and heavy and pounding away at his skull with a blacksmith's hammer.

The brush swept him again—sharp scratches across the top of his head, making him aware of the hammer.

He groaned, squeezing his eyes closed and pressing his cheek hard against his forearm, trying to snuggle deeper into sleep.

A horse's whinny set his eardrums to barking and, in spite of himself, he turned onto a cheek and slitted one eye. The pinto's long, fine snout hung over him, the bristled lips only inches from his face. The horse's breath sounded like the low whistle of air over a bottle neck. The pinto's brown eyes bored into Fargo, as if trying to stare him awake. They glinted copper in the morning sunlight.

Morning?

The Trailsman lifted his head slightly, wincing, and looked around. Crumbling rock walls rose on either side. There was deep grass with a few willows down by an apparent seep. To his left was a cleft in the sloping canyon wall. He was half buried in rocks and gravel at the bottom of the cleft, with a pumpkin-sized rock a few feet away, smeared with dry blood.

He grimaced as consciousness and a millrace of pain and memories of last night—the thunder of the hooves, the shooting, Deana's screams—washed over him.

He glanced at the horse standing a few feet away, looking relieved that its master was still kicking. "Jesus Christ, fella, why the hell didn't you wake me sooner?"

The stallion stared at him skeptically and twitched its ears.

Lifting one hand to his head, the Trailsman felt the dried blood in his hair. The gash didn't feel deep. He'd had concussions before, however, and the unrelenting throbbing told him he had a good one now—nearly drowning out the pain in his arm.

Inspecting the wound Squires had inflicted, he saw that the bandage was soaked with blood, most of it dry. Fortunately, the wound seemed to have clotted some time ago. He pushed himself to his feet, staggering under the searing pain in his head, the ground pitching, and looked around.

The sun was well up, though the air was still cool. Spying his Henry lying half buried in the gravel, he dug it out, brushed it off, levered a fresh shell into the chamber, and headed for the canyon mouth.

He stopped at the edge of the campsite, where he'd left Deana last night, sound asleep in his blankets. The blankets and a few articles of clothing were all that remained of her, the blankets strewn about the fire ring which was heaped with white ashes. The dirt and sand around the fire bore the scuffs and scratches of spurred boots. There was a single, slender print of a bare foot. His camping gear remained where he'd left it.

He turned to peer around a thumb of rock and up the western slope toward Squires's camp. The man's horse was gone but the lean-to tarp flapped in the breeze. No sign of Squires himself.

Cursing, the Trailsman began stumbling down the

grade toward the creek, the pinto following haltingly, sniffing the air and nickering. Fargo stopped after only a few steps and stared stonily toward the cottonwoods, flashing silver in the morning sunshine. Before the trees, the burned hulks of the wagons sagged between tilting, fire-blackened wheels. A couple of thin ribbons of pale smoke wisped from the wreckage.

As he continued slanting across the slope, a guttural sound rose from the other side of a small knoll to Fargo's left. He climbed the knoll and stared down.

Twenty feet away, a brush wolf was hunkered belly-flat, gnawing, a human arm between its paws. It was a slender woman's arm, torn and bloody, with a few inches of a lace-edged calico sleeve clinging to it. The wolf jerked its head up at Fargo, its eyes crossing angrily, and raised its hackles.

The Trailsman lowered the Henry's barrel and fired two quick rounds into the dust before the beast. The wolf yipped, at once terrified and outraged, as it scrambled to its feet in a puff of dust and lunged off toward the creek.

The rifle reports and the smell of the powder smoke made Fargo's head pound harder. What he found farther on down the grade toward the settlers' cold cook fire made his stomach roll, as well. A couple of times, stepping over the bullet-riddled bodies and kicking around the pilgrims' strewn possibles, covering a good seventy square yards, he nearly retched. He had to shoot a couple of the persistent buzzards unwilling to leave their breakfast, and the powder smoke did nothing to settle his stomach.

Apparently, the idiot pilgrims had not yet placed a guard when the marauders attacked. They were all sprawled between the fire and the creek. The women had fled toward the cottonwoods when they'd been shot several times in the back.

Heinze and Haggelthorpe had died with rifles in their hands. Felton had been drilled through his forehead, and only a coffee cup lay near his body, which had been broken and pummeled by horse hooves. Leonard had been shot through the cheek and eyeball.

When Fargo had found the bodies of everyone except for Deana and the Haggelthorpe boys on the bivouac side of the creek, he scoured the brush for a hundred yards upstream and down on the other side.

He felt a fleeting relief when he found nothing but hoof-pounded brush. No sign of Squires, either. The banditos must have taken them. He wasn't sure why they'd taken the boys and Squires, unless they were slave traders, but Deana Dixon was a beautiful woman. It didn't take a genius to figure out why they'd taken her.

Burying the bodies was a slow, tedious job under the hot sun and what felt like an unrelenting crown of thorns. It was a frustrating job, as well, for he felt the minutes ticking past, imagining the gang drifting farther and farther away, Deana and the boys in tow. He should have been on their trail hours ago.

He couldn't leave the pilgrims to the predators, however. Besides, a gang the size of the one the Trailsman had heard from the overhanging ridge would leave a wide swath. He'd follow it. He'd get Deana and the boys back, and he'd make those killers rue the day they'd crossed his path.

Chipping out the single, large grave, he stopped often to bathe his aching head in the creek, then continued hacking at the relatively soft earth near the stream with a pick he'd found only partially burned in one of the wagons. The pinto stood near the water, occasionally glancing up the slope where the raid had occurred, giving a protesting whinny at the smell of carrion, and shaking its head.

When the bodies were buried, Fargo erected a cross formed of driftwood and rawhide straps. He tried to get the cross to stand straight, and gave up after a couple of tries. The burial had been enough. The rocks he'd covered the grave with would keep the predators out.

In spite of the torture several little men with dull chisels were inflicting on his brain plate, it was time to pull his picket pin, and start tracking.

When he'd gathered his gear from the camp fronting the box canyon, he saddled the Ovaro, set his hat gingerly on his tender head, tightened the bandage on his upper left arm, and swung into the leather.

Setting out, he followed the killers' trail east toward town, then south through a broad, shallow valley. He'd been right—they indeed cut a broad swatch. The shod hoof tracks indicated a good fifteen riders, loosely grouped. One of them was dragging a body. Blood and strips of skin splotched the rocks along the grisly furrow cut through the sand and gravel.

Torn bits of a brown wool shirt caught on shrubs and sharp rocks told Fargo the man they were dragging was Squires. Later, a blood-splashed, mule-eared boot leaning against a small boulder confirmed the suspicion. He found the other boot a mile farther up the trail. Larger bits of cloth from the man's shirt, and denim strips from his jeans, began appearing only a few yards ahead.

The trail grew bloodier until he found the poor man himself—what was left of him—belly-down in a shallow wash. Stripped nearly naked, every inch of his body was covered in blood to which sand, gravel, goatheads, and chunks of cholla stuck. Squires's skinned face was unrecognizable, and bare bone shone through the blood and gristle glistening along his arms and legs.

Overhead, buzzards circled as Fargo buried the man on the bank of the wash. The Trailsman muttered a few words over the rock-covered mound, including the promise of vengeance for Squires and his burned town. Then Fargo was astraddle the Ovaro once more, following the broad trail of shod hooves angling southwest toward the purple crags of the Chiricahua Mountains and the misty, mysterious stretches of Old Mexico beyond.

Two hours after burying Squires, he stopped near a seep running out of a rocky scarp only a few yards from the killers' trail. The tracks told him the gang had stopped here, as well.

When he'd loosened the pinto's saddle cinch to give the horse a breather, he grabbed his canteen off his saddle horn, and froze. Something had caught his eye. Holding the canteen low, he strode over to the scarp, and picked up a thin, cotton chemise.

He turned the garment over in his fingers. It had been ripped down the middle. He brought it to his nose and sniffed the faint smell of apple and cherry.

Deana.

His gut filled with fresh bile. He peered pensively up the trail through the heat haze toward a narrow notch between two rimrocks.

If they'd hurt her, they'd soon wish like holy hell they hadn't.

He cursed and dropped the thin garment, then walked over to the seep and filled his canteen. He'd intended on giving the Ovaro a rest, but he and the horse could rest after dark. He could feel the gang slipping away from him, moving closer and closer to the vast desert reaches and devil's playground of the canyons of Old Mexico, and the sun was angling westward. He'd have to take advantage of what little light he had left.

With luck, he'd catch up to them before they crossed the border and he risked being spotted by the Mexican Rurales. Those scattered packs of curly wolves roaming the countryside under the guise of law and order were infamously unkind to foreigners.

But if they did cross, Fargo would cross, too, keeping both eyes skinned on the sudden country around him, his guns loaded and loose in their holsters.

He rode through the rolling desert waste until he was in the cactus-stippled benches of the Chiricahuas—bald upthrusts of jagged sandstone throwing themselves skyward, their northwestern faces turning pink as the sun fell.

Eagles and hawks screeched, and jackrabbits leaped through the chaparral. Coyotes called. When it was too dark to follow the killers' trail in spite of its breadth, Fargo found a low bench on which he'd camped once before out here. After staking the pinto nearby, he allowed himself a low fire of brittle sage branches.

He washed jerky down with coffee, took a few sips from his bottle, then eased back against his saddle, asleep at the end of his first deep breath.

First light found him back on the trail, heading through towering sandstone scarps and rock pillars still silhouetted against the lilac sky in which a few last stars glittered. Around nine, he stopped at another spring. Water was growing scarcer, and he had to take advantage of every drop.

As the pinto drew water under a lone stone ledge, the Trailsman plucked his spy glass from his saddlebags, climbed a scarp, and scanned his back trail—a winding arroyo abutted on both sides by rocks strewn like giant dominoes, with here and there a saguaro or mesquite casting shadows across the orange caliche.

He spread his lips and sucked air through his teeth. About two miles back rose a dust plume. At the head of the plume rode a column of about ten men dressed in light blue and dove gray, and with silver ornaments flashing around their heads.

Rurales.

Fargo hadn't thought he'd crossed into Mexico yet. The uniformed men were on his and the killers' trail. There weren't any *other* horse trails out here.

The Trailsman rode hard the rest of the day and dry-camped in an arroyo, hoping he'd lost his shadowers.

The next morning he was traversing another in a long series of mountain canyons when, stopping to drink from his canteen, the thud of galloping horses rose behind him. At the same time, the Ovaro lifted its head sharply. Fargo lunged forward to grab the pinto's snout, preventing a whinny.

"Easy, boy!"

He cast a glance over his right shoulder. Dust rose from behind a scarp—a thin yellow veil about a hundred yards behind and closing. Men's voices rose on the hot breeze.

Fargo had pushed the Ovaro too hard already; he couldn't outrun the group behind him. Looking around, he saw only rocky buttes and tabletop mesas on both sides of the narrow game trail tracing the canyon floor. Spying a shaded nest of rocks about halfway up the slope on his right, he turned the pinto toward it.

The Ovaro climbed the slope with relative ease, pushing hard with its rear hooves while chopping and lunging with its front. Horse and rider moved up the grade behind a spine of cracked rock. Fifty yards up from the canyon floor, the Trailsman swung out of the saddle and led the horse into a gap between massive, split boulders, tying the reins to a lone ironwood shrub.

He shucked his Henry from the boot and levered a shell as he walked ten yards back down the slope and crouched behind a low, flat-topped boulder. Galloping hooves thudded below, growing louder. He edged a quick peek around the rock.

Seven or eight men in dove gray uniform jackets moved into the canyon from the left, their mustangs and high-stepping Arabians blowing and snorting, the squawk of leather and clank of bridle chains echoing.

The hoof thuds died. Fargo's heart quickened.

He edged another peek around the boulder. Below, the horses had stopped moving forward to mill in a loose group on the canyon floor.

All seven Rurales were looking up the slope toward Fargo, their musket-rifles or pistols raised. Six of the men wore broad-brimmed sombreros sporting the customary silver eagle insignia, while the lead rider—who wore lieutenant's stripes on the gold-stitched, powder blue jacket stretched taut across his bulky frame—had on a leather-billed officer's hat.

The lieutenant and his men were better trackers than Fargo had given them credit for.

With a fateful sigh, Fargo leaped atop the boulder before him and dropped to one knee. All eight men jerked their eyes at him, raising their rifles. Fargo held the Henry across his thigh, ready to raise it if he needed to, and employed his rudimentary Spanish: "Good day, amigos. If you're shadowing me, you're wasting your time. I'm no bandit on either side of the border."

The milling horses snorted. A couple shook their heads. The Rurale privates continued staring up the slope, edgily grasping their rifles and bridle reins while the lieutenant grinned inside his hanging mustaches. His steeldust mare turned a tight circle, its mane jostling.

"El Oso Loco, throw down your weapons! Your trail ends here!"

Before Fargo could work his mind around the name he'd been called, the metallic rasp of a cocking lever sounded behind him. He glanced over his right shoulder.

Spaced out amongst the boulders up the slope behind him, three short, muscular, charcoal-colored men clad in calico tunics and deerskin leggings stared down

76

at him. Two aimed Volcanic Arms lever-action repeaters from their shoulders. The nearest man aimed a Henry with a leather lanyard straight out from his hip, the barrel pointed at Fargo's chest.

The Apache grinned toothlessly.

9

The tribal feathers adorning the Indians' rifle barrels, and the bone-handled knives sheathed on their waists or strapped to their leggings indicated they were Chiricahua Apaches.

No wonder the Rurales had caught up to Fargo so quickly. They had the best guides in the Southwest. Those guides stared at the Trailsman now, their glinting, coffee-colored eyes daring him to lift his rifle.

Fargo turned back toward the Rurales staring up at him, and slowly lowered the Henry to the boulder. The lieutenant laughed. "I thought you would see it my way, El Oso Loco. Now, get your ragged ass down here. You are going to prison, my friend. And then, without a doubt, the firing squad!"

Before Fargo could respond, the lieutenant ordered the three Apaches behind him to lead the prisoner down the hill and to shoot if he tried to escape. The one nearest the Trailsman grunted and muttered in a pidgin Spanish mixed with Chiricahua, indicating Fargo's cartridge belt with his rifle barrel.

When the Trailsman had removed the belt and set it atop the rifle, he leaped down from the boulder, hoping in vain the Apaches wouldn't check his boot for the Arkansas toothpick. But they weren't Apaches for nothing.

Relieved of all his weapons, he was ushered down the hill, the Apaches flanking him on three sides about ten feet away, one leading the Ovaro, their rifles aimed for killing shots.

Below, the Rurales had dismounted. While one private collected the reins of the eight horses, three others scrambled up the slope toward Fargo. The three young Mexicans, barely twenty, approached haltingly, shifting their weight from foot to foot and staring fearfully down their muskets or rifles.

One of them blocked Fargo's path. Holding his hands shoulder high, the Trailsman stopped, cocked a brow at the young man. The young Rurale swallowed nervously and scrambled aside, stumbling over a stone. He and the others fell back as Fargo scrambled the last twenty yards down the hill, bounded off a boulder, and landed on the trail before the lieutenant.

"You're making a mistake," he said, first in Spanish, so the man was sure to understand, then in English, to prove he was a gringo. "I'm not the man you're looking for. Name's Fargo. Skye Fargo."

The lieutenant, holding a big Patterson Colt at Fargo's belly, puffed a fat stogey snugged in one corner of his mouth. He scowled at Fargo from under heavy brows. His fat, sweat-slick face was covered in heavy stubble.

Behind the man rose a loud clattering, and Fargo edged a look around the Rurale lieutenant.

Down the canyon, a wagon crested a rise and started down the other side, heading toward Fargo and the Rurales. It was a barred rig with a roof constructed of brush and chicken wire—a jail wagon. Two young Rurales sat the driver's seat, hoorawing the two mules in the traces. The wagon was a good sixty yards away, but Fargo thought he saw a couple of prisoners slumped in the box.

Fargo looked at the lieutenant, who grinned around his cigar. As the three Apaches and the young Rurales gathered around Fargo as though he were a wounded lion, keeping their rifles aimed at his head and back,

Fargo kept his eyes on their leader. "I'm after the gang that wiped out my wagon train. They—"

"Shut up, El Oso Loco!" the lieutenant snapped, the smile vanishing as he tossed away his cigar. It smacked a rock, showering sparks. He walked toward Fargo, keeping his revolver aimed at the Trailsman's belly. "I'll not listen to any of your bullshit. You're mine, now, you son of a bitch . . . at the end of a very long trail!"

As he said "trail," he jerked the Patterson up and swung the barrel toward Fargo's face, the sharpened foresight angled to slice a cheek. The Trailsman had seen it coming. He ducked as the gun swooped over his head. The lieutenant grunted once with surprise, then again with pain as Fargo buried his right fist in the man's bulging gut.

As the lieutenant stumbled backward, Fargo pivoted. At the same time, a rifle exploded behind him, the slug whistling past his ear and plunking a boulder thirty yards away.

"Don't kill him, goddamn it!" the lieutenant bellowed, gaining his balance, his brown eyes flashing fire. He tightened his jaws. "Just beat the holy *shit* out of him!"

In the corner of his right eye, Fargo saw a young Rurale lunge toward him, jabbing his musket at Fargo's head. The Trailsman parried the blow with his left forearm and smashed his right fist against the young man's jaw. He'd just begun pivoting once more when another rifle butt slammed into his back between his shoulder blades, pounding the air from his lungs. Using the forward momentum, he bulled into an Apache lunging toward him, throwing the smaller man to his back and landing on top of him.

He wrenched the rifle from the Indian's hands. As he whipped around, intending to start shooting because it was the only way to keep his ass out of the oncoming jail wagon, something hard smashed the back of his head.

A half second later, a rifle butt cracked against his jaw. Canyon, Rurales, Apaches, and horses spun around him. Suddenly, all he could hear was the rattling of the jail wagon, as though it were being driven through his ears.

He was slumping sideways when a boot toe separated his ribs. He sucked a breath but hadn't gotten the breath halfway down his throat before another boot, buried deep in his solar plexus, forced it back out.

His last thought before deep night settled inside him was that he hoped they'd take good care of the Ovaro. . . .

He had no idea how long he'd been out before he cracked open his eyes and winced at the bright sunlight pushing between the jail wagon's bars. He lay on his back, staring up at the brush-and-chicken-wire roof.

Beneath him, the boards of the wagon bed lurched and heaved and vibrated as the iron-shod wheels clattered and barked off rocks. The wagon jolted and pitched like a bucking bronc, throwing Fargo onto his shoulder.

He stared across the back of the wagon. Another set of eyes stared back at him, deep-set in a bullet-shaped head. The man lay on his right side, a silver loop ring in his right ear clattering against the wagon bed. His red-and-white-striped shirt was in tatters, as though torn by a sharp whip, and blood shone through the gaps. It pooled on the floorboards beneath his open mouth, from which the man's purple tongue protruded slightly.

The eyes continued staring at Fargo, and the Trailsman was about to say something when he realized the eyes had no light behind them.

He winced at the excruciating pain in his head. If he'd had one railroad spike driven into it before, that spike now had company. His face felt stiff and misshapen. Feeling around with his fingers, he could tell his split lower lip was puffy, and his right eye was swollen to the size of an anthill.

He grabbed the cage's flat iron straps and pulled himself into a sitting position in the right rear corner. He took a deep breath, and, while his ribs ached, he didn't think any were broken.

Before him two other men slumped in opposite corners of the wagon.

The one in the left front corner was a mestizo in leather pants and red shirt, with long, greasy hair, though his scalp was shaved a couple inches above his ears. A leather necklace of bone beads and bear claws flopped on his shirt. He rode with his chin on his chest, head moving to the wagon's pitch and roll.

The other man was a skinny blond gringo with a savage, patch-bearded face. He glared at Fargo, though his lips stretched a smile. He couldn't have been much over twenty, but his eyes were fifty or older and, while he'd been relieved of his weapons, faded patches on both his dusty denim legs bespoke holsters and leather thongs.

Fargo cast his gaze around the wagon, shading his eyes against the sun glare with one hand. They were crossing a rocky flat spotted with isolated brush clumps and saguaros, with stunted cottonwoods pushing up from dry arroyos. Distant rimrocks showed yellow in the heat haze. Two hawks circled what appeared to be an ancient riverbed a half mile away—a deep, dark gash in the rolling desert floor.

The two birds and intermittent dust devils were the only movement in this godforsaken land. Having traversed this corner of Sonora before, guiding freight trains between Tucson and northern Mexican villages, Fargo knew they'd ridden at least twenty miles since the Rurales had captured him, which meant he'd slept through the night.

His heart lifted when he saw the Ovaro plodding along behind him, its reins tied to the cage, its coat dusty and sweat-lathered. Judging by the horse's heavy stride and hanging head, the Mexicans hadn't given it water in some time.

He saw no sign of the lieutenant or most of his men, but two young Rurales rode behind the wagon, about thirty feet back from the dust cloud, their rifles across their saddlebows. A cornhusk cigarette drooped from one of the young men's lips.

The pinto glanced at Fargo, a fleeting, accusatory glance, then looked away, rippling its withers.

"Sorry, fella," the Trailsman muttered. "I'll find a way outta this fix"—he jerked on the cage's rear door, held fast with a heavy padlock, and scowled—"eventually."

"Doubt that."

Fargo turned his head forward. The blond gent was sneering at him.

"You'll be goin' where the rest of us are goin', pard." He stretched his lips back from cracked and broken teeth. "That purty stallion of yourn will be haulin' Lieutenant Rivas's fat ass around. What a shame."

Fargo glanced at the dead man slumped on the other side of the wagon. "You think we oughta tell someone he's passed?"

The blond gent smiled, showing even more bad teeth.

Fargo nodded. "Didn't think so."

For the rest of the day, the wagon hammered across the desert. The Ovaro plodded along behind, tired but ever stalwart. The jostling evoked such a vicious throbbing in the Trailsman's battered head and gut that he aired his paunch twice through the jail wagon's bars. Since he hadn't eaten in many hours, it was mostly a thin green bile that splashed over the shod wheel and onto the dusty trail below.

The blond gent and the two drag-riding Rurales laughed. The Ovaro whinnied.

Fargo ran a sleeve across his mouth and shrugged. He slumped into the wagon's right rear corner, closed his eyes, and in spite of the wagon's ceaseless hammering, felt sleep wash over him like a hot wave of water.

The hammering entered his dreams. So did the clomps of horse hooves, a screech of dry wagon wheels, and the voices of Lieutenant Rivas and the other Rurales.

Then, vaguely, as if his blind consciousness were perched atop a high mountain and merely half aware of what was happening to his body, he felt the hammer stop.

Other voices intruded on that of Rivas. Fargo felt himself being half dragged, half carried up steps. Suddenly, there was a warm rain. Just as suddenly, a cold winter's evening settled into his bones and his teeth clattered.

The clattering ceased. There was a girl's muffled giggle. The Trailsman felt a pleasant tingling at the base of his belly, a stirring in his loins.

He felt himself rising slowly, as if from deep in a warm seabed. He cracked his eyes open. Far above stretched a broad ceiling in a herringbone pattern of boards. His eyelids fluttering, the Trailsman lowered his gaze slightly.

A black-haired girl knelt beside him on a massive bed. She was naked, and her hair hung down to hide her face as she caressed his chest with a wet sponge.

Another girl knelt by his left hip. She, too, was naked. Between her hands jutted Fargo's erect member.

Slowly, she bent over his belly, her full breasts sloping down from her chest and between the curtains of her thick, black hair. Her russet skin shone in the light from a nearby fire as she lowered her head to his crotch and touched the tip of her tongue to the head of his swollen shaft.

Fargo felt a fire rage inside him as the girl flicked her tongue from left to right upon the throbbing head. As, with infinite, excruciating slowness, she slid her warm, wet mouth down over his length, he sucked a deep breath, arched his back, and gripped the sheets with his fists.

She took him as far down as she could, gagging slightly, her throat expanding and contracting around the head of his shaft. Then she lifted her mouth slowly, keeping her lips taut against him.

When she came to the end, she planted a tender kiss on the tip, then lowered her mouth once more, repeating the process and increasing the pace until Fargo gave a guttural grunt and let go, nearly tearing the sheet from the bed and grinding his heels into the mattress.

When his seed had finished jetting down the girl's opening and closing throat, he relaxed and opened his eyes. The girl to his right dropped her sponge in the wooden bowl beside her and smiled down at him, her molasses-colored eyes flashing in the firelight.

She lowered her head and kissed him, her lips warm and supple. "You better now, *hombre grande*?"

Fargo cleared his throat. "N-not to sound ungrateful or anything, but . . . who the hell *are* you and where the hell *am* I?"

10

Senorita Diablo sat the white barb in the shade of a volcanic scarp overhanging the trail, drew her long, black cigarillo to her lips, and inhaled deeply. As she blew out the smoke, she stared down the trail undulating through the blond, sun-scorched, yucca-studded hills.

Two hundred yards away, a village nestled in a broad valley—two dozen or so bone white adobes with here and there a mud-brick, brush-roofed shack and stable. An adobe mission cathedral stood like a giant, sandstone monolith in the cobbled plaza, at the far end, thrusting a stout wooden cross at the sky.

A thin mare's trail of dust rose between the senorita and the village. Presently, two straw sombreros bobbed along a hill crest, pushed up by the two heads before the shoulders and torsos of the two gang members appeared, men and horses cresting the rise then trotting leisurely down the other side.

The senorita turned toward the group flanking her—her own men, standing in the shade of the overhang, drinking from canteens or smoking, and talking desultorily. Directly behind the senorita, the blond gringa sat a stout, dark brown mule, her back erect, wan face downcast, wrists lashed to her saddle horn.

She wore one of the senorita's calico blouses, the tails untucked. Her gold-blond hair, dusty and seed-flecked, hung like a soiled curtain about her pretty, fine-boned face.

To the gringa's right, the two boys sat their own mule, the tallest one ahead of the other, who slept with his head against his older brother's back. The tall boy stared stonily into the *poblado* below, his sunburned cheeks peeling and his lips cracked from the beating El Oso Loco had given him when he and his brother tried to escape their camp two nights ago. The boys were tied together with ropes around their waists, their feet lashed beneath the mule's belly.

All three of the senorita's prisoners had made the three-day trip from the border in good shape. They would bring good money from the agents who ran the gold mine in St. Augustin to the south.

"Mount up!" she called as the two riders approached, hooves thudding.

As El Oso Loco and the mestizo, Dominguez, approached, "the crazy bear" lifted his black sombrero and ran an arm across his heavily bearded face, the blind eye appearing nearly opaque in the sunlight. The beads on his deerskin vest flashed like jewels in the high-altitude sunlight.

"All clear, *chiquita*. No Rurales, no *soldados*. Just the usual banditos and campesinos with a few vaqueros drinking themselves silly in the cantinas. Anselmo reports that he and Magdelena recently finished a fresh tub of *baconora*. Our spirits will be soaring this evening!"

"Sí, our spirits will soar this evening," the senorita said, putting the steel to her barb and lunging off down the trail, jerking the blonde's mule along behind her. "But if Anselmo has not yet changed his recipe, tomorrow we may very well be *blind*!"

She'd traversed three hogbacks when the *poblado*'s outlying shacks began pushing up on both sides of the trail. As she cleaved the narrow main street between the hunched, cracked adobes baking in the desert sun, dogs began barking and gaudily dressed and painted whores began shouting from balconies. El Oso Loco and the other men responded by whooping and hollering and firing their pistols into the air.

The small-time banditos and desert prospectors, smoking and drinking under brush arbors, whistled and clapped, beckoning and offering to buy Senorita Diablo a drink.

"Over here, Senorita!" came a shout from the right side of the street. She turned to see a peg-legged stableman propped on his pitchfork by a dilapidated hay wagon, smiling at her broadly. "No man can satisfy you like I can! Bring your gringa friend. A man with my vitality can satisfy two women at once!"

El Oso Loco rode up to the right of Senorita Diablo and turned toward the stableman. "You think so, Paco? Here—see how well you can satisfy two women without your balls!"

El Oso Loco's Dragoon belched smoke and fire. A wedge of slivers blew out of the stableman's wooden leg, about knee-high. With a yelp, the stableman wheeled awkwardly and hobbled into his green-doored stable, the goats in his pen bleating raucously and running in circles.

"Sorry, I missed!" bellowed El Oso Loco, triggering another shot as the stableman pulled the doors closed behind him.

"Pig!" Senorita Diablo scolded her lover as she dropped smoothly out of her saddle before a broad, two-story adobe hotel with arched windows and wrought-iron balconies on the second floor. Her calf-skin chaps flapped about her legs as she strode onto the boardwalk before the building—second in size only to the cathedral in this town. "He's more man than you will ever be!"

El Oso Loco dismounted and raised his voice above

the gunfire behind him, the rest of the gang still showing off for the *putas.* "How would you know?"

"You weren't the first, El Oso Loco!" The senorita
laughed. Standing on the edge of the raised boardwalk
while he remained in the street, she flicked his hat
down his back, grabbed his shirt in both her fists,
pulled him toward her brusquely, and kissed him.
"And you certainly will not be the last!"

"You, either, you devilish little bitch!" El Oso Loco
tried to pull her back, but she sidestepped him and
ducked under the hitch rack.

"Lock the boys in the hotel stable, but chase out
the snakes and scorpions first!" With a husky laugh,
the senorita strode up to the mule on which the
blonde sat, crouched defensively against the rough-
housing in the street behind her.

El Oso Loco had led the mule carrying the two boys
into town. The mule was skitter-stepping at the pistol
fire, both boys flinching at the shots, the younger one
howling and beseeching his brother to do something.
El Oso Loco laughed, grabbed the lead rope, and
began leading the mule across the square toward the
cathedral looming beyond the dry stone fountain.

"Pretty yourself up for me, Senorita!" he called behind him, both boys cowering from the gunfire. "It's
been a long ride, and I will be back to take my
pleasure!"

"Only after you bathe, you pig!"

Senorita Diablo jerked the blonde's mule up to the
boardwalk, and looped the rope over the hitch rack.
"You behave yourself, gringa, and you will have a nice
hotel room to luxuriate in before we sell you to the
miners. If you try to escape, I will throw you in the
stable with the young gringos and the black widow
spiders."

As she cut the blonde's hands free of the saddle
horn with her bone-handled folding knife, the gringa

said tightly, as if fighting hysteria, "I am no whore. Please let me go."

Senorita Diablo threw her head back on her shoulders, her thick black hair cascading down her back. "You may be no whore now, but when those lonely miners in St. Augustin set their eyes on you . . . and their hands . . . you will be a whore soon enough!"

"What do you need the money for?"

Senorita Diablo looked up at the blonde who was staring down at her with genuine curiosity. The senorita pulled the gringa out of the saddle and faced her, smiling. "For rifles, of course. Food, tequila, horse shoes, ammunition—what else is there?" She gave the blonde a shove toward the hotel's batwing doors. "Now, get in there and get your beauty sleep. You have only a short time to rest before we pretty you up and send you to St. Augustin!"

Senorita Diablo locked the blonde, whose name she had learned was Deana Dixon, in a room directly across the hall from her own. A rare generosity touched her, and in addition to having her own bath brought up to her room by the hotel owner, she had one brought up to Deana Dixon's room, as well.

The senorita enjoyed her bath thoroughly while smoking a fresh cigarillo, drinking sangria from a straw-basketed jug, and listening to the festive guitar and piano music rising from the street. The afternoon waned toward evening, with the sunlight softening and shadows growing. There were occasional whoops and pistol shots around the little town, but the revelry had generally taken a more sedate tone, most of the banditos having retired to the whores' cribs and dusky cantinas.

Finished with her bath, the senorita drew a silk wrapper around her shoulders, letting it hang open at the front, and stood at the open window, letting the dry, cool air caress her skin.

She was ready for some of that loving now, herself, but having turned El Oso Loco away until he'd bathed meant she'd have to wait until tomorrow. She could hear him down there in one of the cantinas, singing the old song about the sheepherder and the Spanish princess at the top of his lungs.

Senorita Diablo sneered. Spanish princess. What a crock of goatshit!

She took a swig from the cool stone jug, enjoying the taste of the sweet, fruity wine in her throat after so many days on the trail. She savored the last, long drag off her cigarillo, flicked it through the window, watched it spark out in the street below, and then turned and moved to the door.

Time to make sure that Deana Dixon hadn't found a way out of her room. . . .

She grabbed the key off the washbasin and stepped into the hall, holding her wrapper closed at her waist. She slid the key into the lock of the opposite door, turned it quietly, thrust the door open two feet, and poked her head inside.

There was a startled cry and a splash of water. Standing in the small, copper tub, Deana Dixon turned toward the senorita while crossing her arms on her chest, her wet, naked breasts bulging out around her elbows. Her hair was down, falling in gold-blond ringlets about her narrow shoulders. The shutter was closed and locked, but daylight pushed through the cracks between the boards. A candle burned in a bottle atop the washbasin.

"You might try knocking!"

"Just making sure you're still here."

The blonde's lustrous brown eyes were incriminating. "If I somehow managed to escape, where would I go?"

Senorita Diablo smiled as she stepped into the room and pressed her back against the door, latching it. "Good point."

"Get out."

"Don't get sassy, bitch. Your life is in my hands."

"What . . . and deliver a corpse to the miners in St. Augustin?"

Senorita Diablo smiled again as she strode toward the tub, her lips rolling even more than usual under the influence of the sangria. "You have sand. How rare in a high-bred gringa. A lady!" Her eyes dropped slowly along Deana Dixon's flared hips and long legs, and the triangular tuft of honey-blond fur between her thighs. "A nice figure, too."

"I'll bring in much lucre for your rifles."

The senorita held up the sangria. "Drink?"

The girl stared back at her, frowning slightly.

Senorita Diablo laughed and lifted the wine to her lips, letting a little dribble down both corners of her mouth. She swallowed and let her eyes roam across the gringa's crossed arms, the crescents of her damp breasts peeking out from under each elbow.

Suddenly, the bandita lurched forward, clamping a hand on the back of the gringa's neck and pressing their mouths together. Deana Dixon gave a startled cry and tried to pull away. Senorita Diablo held her firm, mashing her lips against the blonde's, whose tongue recoiled toward the back of her mouth as the gringa's slithered toward it.

Laughing, the bandita dropped her hand from the blonde's neck, and pulled away. "Maybe later, huh?"

The blonde glared at her, cheeks flushed with fury. She held only one arm across her breasts while the other held an edge of the dresser flanking the tub. The senorita pulled the gringa's arm away from her chest and stared down at the pale, full breasts, her eyes smoky. She palmed the left breast, kneading it brusquely and pinching the nipple.

"Yes," said Senorita Diablo. "Maybe later."

She turned and, feeling sensual with her breasts swaying freely under the open wrapper, sauntered toward the door. She took another deep pull from the flask, opened the door, stepped out, and drew it closed behind her.

The bolt clicked as she locked it.

Back in her room, the senorita considered dressing and joining the revelers in the street. But what was the point? Though it was early in the evening, her men were all three sheets to the wind. None could even hold their own in a card game.

Also, she was tired from the long ride.

She sat up for a time, cleaning her guns and sharpening her knives while she drank the sangria and listened to the laughter, singing, and guitar chords rising from the cantinas, then blew out the lamp and crawled between the bed's coarse sheets.

She wasn't sure how much time had passed before her eyes snapped open. She lay with her head on the pillow, staring into the darkness, listening.

A murmur rose from across the hall. A man's voice sounded, low and taut with anger. Spurs chinged faintly. A sharp slap was followed by a muffled sob.

Senorita Diablo flung the sheets back and dropped her long legs to the floor, grabbing a .32 revolver from the stand beside her bed. She plucked her wrapper off a chair back, drew it on without tying it, and opened the door.

Wan amber light shone beneath the door on the other side of the dark hall. Bedsprings squeaked as men whispered.

Senorita Diablo placed her hand on the doorknob and turned it slowly. It wasn't locked. When the latch clicked, she flung the door wide and took two steps forward, the wrapper wafting open as she raised the cocked Allen and Wheelock straight out in her right hand, swinging it back and forth between the two men in the room.

One stood beside the bed, a pistol in his right hand, facing the naked blonde who lay on her back, legs spread. Another man, his black pants and underwear pulled down around his spurred boots, lay between the blonde's bent knees, holding her hands down on both sides of her pillow. His swollen member jutted between his legs.

The two men jerked their heads toward the open door, eyes snapping wide. A couple of shitty-smelling vaqueros whom the senorita had seen in town from time to time, always drunk and chasing the cheapest whores.

"Senorita!" both men exclaimed at the same time.

For stretched seconds, all four people in the room froze as though for a photograph, the blonde and the two men staring at the senorita in the open doorway, the senorita staring back, a hard smile on her lips, a cold light in her eyes. The man standing by the bed turned, slowly swinging his cocked pistol toward the senorita but keeping it low.

"Senorita," he said, his eyes rheumy from drink, "please, we were only trying to satisfy ourselves . . ."

Remaining frozen between the blonde's spread legs, her naked breasts rising and falling beneath him, the other man said softly, "Please, Senorita . . . we beg your mercy."

The senorita stepped forward, aiming her cocked revolver at the man on the bed. "If mercy is what you want . . . you'll have to look for it elsewhere."

She swung the revolver toward the man standing to her left and fired, the report rocking the room and making the lantern flame gutter.

The bullet drilled a neat, round hole through the standing man's forehead. As he gave a clipped scream and, dropping his own pistol, flew back against the bed's left front post, the senorita cocked the smoking revolver once more and swung it back toward the man on the bed.

"No!" the man wailed, rising and spreading his arms, mouth and eyes drawn wide with horror.

The senorita's revolver spoke twice, smoke wafting through the room. The bullets plunked through the man's chest and into the wall behind him, splattering blood across the plaster.

He screamed and flew backward off the bed, hitting the floor between the bed and the wall with a thunderous crash. The shudder of thrashing limbs gradually faded to silence.

In the street, a whore laughed above somnolent guitar twangs. Footsteps shuffled in the hall.

The senorita looked at the blonde, who lay curled on her side, staring at the dead man on the floor in front of the bed. Her body trembled.

The senorita strode forward, stopped beside the bed, and smoothed a lock of hair back from the blonde's right temple. "Maybe I don't seem so unpleasant, now, huh?"

"Senorita!" a voice sounded in the doorway behind her.

Staring down at the blonde, the senorita bunched her lips with disgust. "Thank God I'll be rid of you in a couple days."

She turned to see a little mustachioed man in the doorway, wearing a shabby wool vest and a soiled apron, casting a terrified glance about the room. Closing her wrapper over her breasts, she moved toward him.

"Haul the bodies out to the nearest trash heap, Frederico," the senorita ordered. "And if you give out any more keys to this room—no matter how much they threaten you—I'll gouge your eyes out with my thumbs."

With that she strode back to her room and slammed the door.

"*Sí, Senorita,*" muttered the little man in the doorway.

11

The multitalented young Mexican girls in the Trails-man's bed convinced him without much effort that he had no need to know who they were or where he was just then. Those answers would come in due time. For now, it was best that they helped him relax, heal, and sleep.

He slept with the girls curled around him, limbs entwined with his. A long, blissful, healing sleep.

Birdsong woke him. Opening his eyes, he saw golden sunlight angling through the cracks between the window shutters. A branch waved outside the shutter, flicking a shadow across a smooth, brown thigh angled over his right leg. The other girl slept with her head on his belly, lips parted as she breathed, naked shoulders rising and falling gently. Her breath was warm and moist against his skin.

So, he hadn't been hallucinating. He'd been doctored by two of the loveliest medicos in the territory, no doubt.

Outside rose the sharp clanks of a blacksmith's hammer, forcing him back to reality and the questions: Where was he? Whose place was this? Who were these girls sleeping around him like brown-skinned desert sprites?

He reached down, ran his hand across the shoulder of the girl asleep on his belly. Gently, he smoothed her hair back from her eyes. She groaned as she slid her head off his belly, rolling over and curling up, her back pressed against his side. Pushing up on his elbows, he scooted down toward the end of the bed, sliding out from under the other girl's leg without waking her, then dropped his feet to the floor.

Resting his elbows on his thighs, he took his head in his hands, and felt a bandage wound tightly across his forehead and tied firmly in back. It felt dry. His head was tender, but the excruciating pain he'd felt before was gone. There was only a dull ringing in his ears. His lip, eye, and jaw still ached, however. His fingers discovered that his right eye was still swollen, and the burning cut in his lower lip was on the mend.

He looked around and found his clothes on a high-backed chair near the bed—everything but his hat and boots freshly laundered. His hat had been brushed, and his gun belt oiled. Even his Henry, standing in a corner of the thick-adobe-walled room, had been cleaned and buffed till the walnut stock and brass receiver fairly glistened in a shaft of light angling through a shutter.

He dressed quietly while the girls breathed softly on the bed behind him. When he'd donned his hat and knotted his neckerchief, he carried his spurred boots to the heavy, double oak doors. He opened one door by its ornate latch handle and peered into a dimly lit hall.

Spying no one and hearing nothing but birds from outside, he went out, closed the door gently, and stepped into his boots.

Hefting his Henry, he looked around. More light shone on his right than his left in the cavernous hall, so he began walking toward the light, stepping quietly, his spurs ringing lightly on the stone floor. As the light grew he was able to more clearly see the large, gilt-framed paintings on the walls around him, the occasional conquistador's shield, sword, or helmet, or a stone sculpture of dogs and horses.

While the furnishings were rich, there was a shabby aspect to the place. Everything was covered in dust. The walls bore long cracks, and the stone floor was damp and bulging in places, as though from water pushing up from underground—the result of a dilapidated drainage system, no doubt.

At the end of the hall, he came to a courtyard lined with pillars and overgrown with brown brush, ancient vines climbing the pillars and walls. A statue fountain depicting a robed priest and a large, panting dog hadn't seen water in years. Its cracked bowl was filled with dust and leaves.

A loud clang sounded on the other side of the courtyard, followed by a shouted Spanish curse. From a stone chimney jutting from the tiled roof opposite, blue smoke wafted, filling the courtyard with the smell of spiced meat and tortillas. The Trailsman's mouth watered as he walked along the courtyard, his boots clomping, churs ringing off the cobbles, and followed another hall inside, toward the voices growing louder before him.

He was about to turn the corner into a brightly lit room when a stocky black dog, a mastiff, bounded out from a massive table, barking and growling and showing its teeth. It lunged toward Fargo threateningly, when the man sitting at the table's far end clapped his hands twice, the slaps echoing around the room's thick walls and a vaulted ceiling with the same herringbone pattern of slats and beams as Fargo's bedroom.

"Heel, Paquito, heel!" the man ordered in Spanish.

When the dog only stopped lunging, but continued to bark and raise its hackles, the Spanish man, who had a cloth bib hanging from the collar of his short *chucca* jacket, threw a spoon. Missing the dog by a good foot, the spoon hit the wall to Fargo's right, ringing loudly before clattering onto the stone-tiled floor.

The dog jerked a look at its master, growling low

in its throat, then glanced back at the Trailsman once more, licking its chops, before turning and slinking off to a corner in which lay a fur-matted red cushion and pie pan filled with water.

"Senor Fargo, I do apologize for the rude greeting," the man said in near-perfect English, beaming up at the Trailsman, black eyes glistening. He indicated one of the high-backed chairs facing the table. "Won't you join me? I've already eaten with my men, but I will sit with you while you enjoy Fernando's lamb."

Without waiting for a response, the old gent raised his hands to his right shoulder, and clapped three times. "Fernando, our guest has arisen. Another plate, if you please!"

"Sí, Sí," came a voice from beyond two stout wooden doors standing open behind the old Mexican. *"Estaré allí en un minuto!"*

"Please, please!" said the old Mexican, indicating a chair. "Sit down, amigo. Take a load off!"

The Trailsman pulled out a leather-cushioned, scrolled-wood chair three chairs down from the table's end, regarding the old Mexican speculatively. The fancy albeit neglected digs and the man's regal attire—a black Spanish-cut suit with gold stitching, which he'd become too small for, leaving the shoulders too wide—bespoke a landowner, but Fargo couldn't remember seeing him before.

"I'm afraid you have the advantage, Senor . . ."

"De la Garza. Don Eduarto Ramón de la Garza. Don't worry. Your mind is not gone. We never met officially, but you were pointed out to me several years ago, on a Mississippi riverboat."

The don reached into his suit coat to pluck a fat cigar from the pocket of his white linen shirt. "I had taken one of my daughters to New Orleans . . . for some *Americano* culture . . . and we decided to go up the river a ways. You and a lovely gringa boarded the boat in a most unconventional fashion. You swam out from shore, with men shooting at you. The boat wasn't as safe a refuge as you'd thought, however. From an upper deck I watched you fight off five men who'd been harassing the girl."

The old man grinned as he bit off the cigar's end, showing large, yellow teeth inlaid with gold. "It was quite a spectacle. You took down five men in five minutes with only your fists and an Arkansas toothpick. The captain, an old friend, told me who you were. I guess you could say I have been an admirer of yours ever since."

"I apologize for not remembering you. But I *do* remember having my hands full during that little jaunt down the Miss." Fargo leaned forward, shoving a scrap-littered plate out of his way. By the number of plates and stone mugs on the table, it appeared that five men in addition to the don had recently breakfasted. "Another thing I don't remember is how in the hell I ended up *here.*"

He looked around at the long table, at a living room, glimpsed through an open door to his left, in which heavy wooden furniture was arranged before a massive fieldstone hearth. Beyond the tall, open windows before him was a broad patio filled with unpruned fruit trees. Beyond that lay a low stone wall, crumbling in places and bordering a broad yard in which adobe outbuildings, including barns and stables, sat forlornly in the unchecked scrub.

The yard shone pallid and dusty in the midmorning light. He half expected to see the Rurales milling about somewhere. But not a soul stirred. Jays cawed in the pecan trees shading a springhouse. A single cottontail rabbit sat nibbling the grass growing tall at a corner of a low, double-doored adobe—probably a blacksmith shop, with shuttered windows and a falling-down brush arbor.

The don opened his mouth to respond to the Trailsman's question, but stopped and turned when spurred boots clanged and clomped behind him. Fargo saw a squat, round-faced Mexican move out from the double doors at the rear of the room, carrying a wooden tray on his right shoulder.

The man looked more like a field hand than a cook in his stained burlap shirt and baggy denim trousers, secured beneath his paunch with a worn leather belt. A red neckerchief was knotted around his neck. His greasy hair hung in his eyes, which were spoked with smile lines, and his scraggly mustache hung down over both sides of his mouth, the corners of which quirked upward as he approached the table to Fargo's right.

"Senor Fargo, meet my *el segundo* and, since my kitchen help left me a little over a year ago, chief cook and"—he paused and looked around as if for the right English expression—"*bottle washer*—Fernando Sandoval."

"*Sí, sí,*" the paunchy Mexican said, shaking Fargo's hand. His Spanish was too fast for the Trailsman to follow clearly, but he said something about being honored. He apologized for the meager breakfast—though Fargo considered roasted lamb, frijoles, corn, tortillas, and syrup far from meager. He said so in broken Spanish as the old vaquero bowed and, holding his serving tray flat against his chest, ambled back into the kitchen.

"Many thanks for the spread," Fargo said, looking down at the three plates and a steaming stone coffee mug spread out before him. "And, thanks also, for your . . . uh . . . *medical* services."

De la Garza laughed, throwing his head back on his shoulders as the Trailsman filled a tortilla with corn and lamb. "You are most welcome, Senor. The ship's captain told me that, on occasion, you were known to enjoy the company of the fairer sex. When you rode in here three nights ago, you looked so poorly that I, too, nearly mistook you for El Oso Loco. I thought that if you were to have a fighting chance at life, those two little *chiquitas*—well, *putas*, to be precise—would be the ones to give it to you. They live in a nearby village, and I enjoy their services from time to time, myself. Orphans, both. Their mother was an Apache medicine witch, and I believe a little of her talent has worn off—don't you agree?"

The Trailsman spoke around a mouthful of food, feeling his face warm. "They're right bewitching, I'll give them that." He chewed, swallowed, and glanced at the don as he lifted his coffee mug. "But how did you get me out of that jail wagon in the first place?"

"The Rurales always pass this way, looking for banditos—so many since the drought has hit this side of the mountains, making it difficult for the campesinos to earn an honest living. Lieutenant Veras and I drink tequila together and"—the don's gaze grew pensive, his expression dark—"discuss certain aspects of the banditos which I have a special interest in—namely El Oso Loco and, sadly, my own daughter."

He puffed his cigar quietly for a time, sitting back in his chair and staring out a window.

Continuing, he said with a fateful sigh, "The major thought he had finally caught the infamous El Oso Loco when, in fact, it was you. I had his men carry you out of the wagon and put you in one of my rooms. Your horse, the magnificent Ovaro, is in my stable. Fernando has tended him well."

After mentioning his daughter, the don's expression had remained dark, his eyes downcast, his tone grim. Absently, he puffed his cigar and studied his coffee mug.

"Much obliged for the tending of me and my horse," Fargo said. "And I'm sorry about your daughter. It so happens I have my own interest in El Oso Loco. I'll be pulling foot soon."

De la Garza turned to him sharply, smoke streaming from his nostrils. "What is your interest in El Oso Loco, Senor Fargo?"

Fargo swallowed another mouthful of food, swabbing his nearly clean plate with a tortilla scrap. His own tone was sharp. "He wiped out a group of pilgrims I'd piloted to Bone Creek Canyon in Arizona. Butchered them and left their bodies to the coyotes. Looted and burned their wagons. Took a girl and two boys." He shoved the syrup-drenched tortilla into his mouth. "I was trailing him when the Rurales caught up to me."

The don studied him thoughtfully, eyes darting around in their sockets, thin blue cigar smoke curling up around his face. He said with a wistful air, "If you are trailing El Oso Loco, Senor Fargo, you are trailing my daughter, as well. . . ."

Fargo looked at him, chewing.

The don cleared his throat and said through a sigh, "She has ridden with him these past three years. It is a grave dishonor for me, of course, and her dear, dead mother. Thank God her three sisters, well married in Mexico City, do not have to endure it."

Fargo shoved his spotless plate away and hooked a finger through his coffee mug. "Forgive me for asking, but how did your daughter hook up with a killer like El Oso Loco?"

"You could just as easily ask, Senor, how El Oso Loco hooked up with her." The don planted his hands on the table and stood with considerable effort, grunting and frowning and breathing hard. He grabbed a cane hooked by its silver horse head over the edge of the table to his right, and rose, shoving the chair back with his legs. Leaning on the cane, he limped—it was more of a shuffle, with the right leg unbending at the knee—to one of the open windows. His back to the room, he leaned his right shoulder against the shutter and lifted the cigar to his mouth. Smoke puffed around his head.

So obviously dark were the man's thoughts that they seemed to dull the sunlight in the yard beyond the patio, as though a cloud had passed over the sun.

"An evil one, she," de la Garza continued, in a voice almost too low for the Trailsman to hear. "We tried everything, Doña Anna and myself, to make her feel loved, to show her tenderness so that she would show tenderness to others. Instead, she was a cruel, angry child—as incorrigible as she was beautiful. Of course, having men around the hacienda—young men whose heads she could easily turn—didn't lessen our problems. Then, suddenly, when she was seventeen, she took up with El Oso Loco, a bandito who had been rustling my cattle and driving them to Agua Prieta.

"I confronted her in the village, forbade her to see him, and she pulled a gun on me. She shot me in both legs. The left one broke the bone but did no lasting damage." The don tapped his right shin with his cane. "The other one shattered my knee. She would have left me to bleed to death in an alley beyond a *whorehouse* if Fernando had not heard the shots."

Fargo dropped his eyes to the coffee mug, which he held in both hands. In the upper periphery of his vision, he saw the don turn his head to him, lips bunched with fury. "If you find her, Senor Fargo, I will pay you five hundred dollars—it is all I can afford in these lean times—to *kill* her!"

Fargo frowned across the table at the man.

"It sounds harsh," the don continued, slowly swinging his head back toward the window. "But I do not think only about myself. She has killed many innocent people. I brought her into this world, thus I should be the one to take her out of it—even if I have to pay someone to do it."

The Trailsman slid his chair out from the table and stood uncertainly, still a little wobbly. "I'm sorry about your trouble, Don, but I'm not a hired gunman. If she's in the group that killed my people, she'll die, just as El Oso Loco will die . . . and anyone else responsible. I won't take a dime for doing what's right."

"Be careful. Not even the Rurales will go near the *poblado* in which she and El Oso Loco hole up when they are not rampaging along the border." De la Garza shook his head slowly. "It is the home of many bad hombres."

The Trailsman donned his hat, adjusting it over the bandage. "Thanks for the breakfast. If you don't mind, I think I'll rest here another day, and leave first thing in the morning. I'd appreciate a map to this *poblado* your daughter and El Oso Loco hole up in."

"Stay as long as you want, Senor Fargo. I will draw you a detailed map."

"Obliged. Now I think I'll check on my horse."

"There's a door through there," the don said, pointing toward the large, cavernous living room shrouded in darkness to Fargo's left.

Fargo strode toward it, spurs chinging across the tiles. Behind him, standing at the window, the don puffed his cigar and stared at the Trailsman's broad, buckskin-clad back fading into the shadows.

12

When the Trailsman had found the Ovaro contentedly foraging in a large paddock shaded by oaks and mesquite, a small spring freshet running through it, he returned to his room for a long, solitary nap.

He was wandering the dilapidated hacienda grounds, with their sunbaked fields and abandoned buildings, when the don sent the girls for him. He and de la Garza played two-handed poker for the rest of the day on the weathered patio off the dining room.

That night, Fernando roasted a wild javelina, and Fargo, de la Garza, the cook, and de la Garza's five remaining vaqueros ate on the patio under the stars, by the light of the roasting fire, with the cool night falling heavily and meteors sparking over the mountains.

Later, someone played a guitar. While the men drank brandy and smoked cigars, the girls, whose names were Helena and Marguerita, danced amorously around the fire.

Only one of the girls joined the Trailsman in his room later—the other no doubt attending the don. Fargo and Helena, drunk on brandy and wine and the enchanted Old Mexican night, made sweet, passionate love on the sprawling bed before collapsing into each other's arms.

"Are you sure you will not let me find you some pistoleros in the village?" the don asked the next morning, standing in the yard outside the massive casa as Fargo swung up into the pinto's hurricane deck. The yard was filled with cool, blue shadows, the sun not yet having crested the eastern mountains. "My daughter and El Oso Loco have many men riding with them. Seasoned banditos. *Muy* bad *hombres*."

"Sometimes one man has a better chance than a few," Fargo said. "I'll go it alone, but I much appreciate the map . . . and, uh, your sundry *other* kindnesses."

"You should at least shave. Your beard adds to your uncanny likeness to El Oso Loco."

Fargo ran his hand down his four-day growth of beard, which he'd grown intentionally. He hoped that, when he crossed paths with El Oso Loco, their similar appearances would give the bandito pause enough for the Trailsman to get the drop on him. "That's what's I'm counting on."

Leaning on his silver-headed cane, de la Garza shook the Trailsman's hand and peered meaningfully into Fargo's eyes. "Let me know how your endeavor turns out, *por favor*."

The Trailsman flicked his hat brim and reined the Ovaro around. "You got it." He heeled the horse into a southwestward gallop through the cottonwoods, across the spindly creek, and into the cool, blue, ridge-relieved distances beyond the sprawling hacienda.

The next day, late in the afternoon, he hunkered down in a nest of boulders rammed up against the base of a tongue-shaped scarp, and lifted his spyglass to his right eye. He winced as sand blown by a wind that had picked up around noon, and which showed no sign of relenting, pelted the rocks around him.

He adjusted the focus as he aimed the glass down the steep slope and across several low, brush-covered hogbacks across which the sand-whipping wind moaned, bowing the shrubs. Where the hogbacks rolled out into a narrow, flat valley, the *poblado* of La Escondida hunkered, the white pueblos obscured by the buffeting sand curtains.

He scrutinized the village for some time, occasionally lowering the spyglass to blow grit from the lens. Satisfied he had a general sense of the layout, he reduced the glass, doffed his hat, and removed the bandage Helena and Marguerita had wrapped around his head. His plan for locating Deana Dixon and the Haggelthorpe boys—if they were still alive and in the village, that was—was to try and finagle his way into the bandit gang. He'd have had an easier chance of not getting shot in the process if he could pass for Mexican, but his Spanish wasn't good enough.

Instead, he'd have to pass as an American border tough—one tough enough that he'd be a worthy comrade to El Oso Loco and Senorita Diablo, as the don's daughter called herself—but not so tough that he'd piss them off and draw a bullet. He'd be walking a thin line in hostile territory, but he could think of no other way to free the survivors of the wagon train massacre.

Letting the wind take the bandage, he tramped through the boulders to the Ovaro waiting on the other side of the rocky hill, returned the spyglass to his saddlebags, mounted up, and turned the horse back onto the trail.

Ten minutes later, as he descended the last hogback, the scraggly shacks and stables began closing on both sides of the trail, the smell of goat dung and over-overfilled latrines wafting on the breeze.

The village hunkered down in silence against the thrashing wind, most of the shutters closed over windows. Tumbleweeds crisscrossed the narrow, cobbled street, pasting themselves against stock troughs and boardwalks and awning posts. Several had lodged in second-story balconies.

The weather hadn't kept everyone inside. Several men in outlandishly broad-brimmed sombreros sat under brush arbors fronting cantinas. They watched Fargo with interest as he passed along the street, hunkered low against the wind, holding his hat on his head with one hand.

When a livery barn appeared on his left, both doors open to the street, he pulled the Ovaro into the musty shadows, crouching through the low doorframe, and stopped. Beneath the braying wind and creaking rafters, there was the sound of broken liquid streams hitting a wooden bucket. His eyes adjusted to the shadows as he looked around the barn.

A cow stood to his left, head facing the right wall. A three-legged stool sat on the other side of the cow, a man in rope sandals and coarse white trousers straddling it. With one hand he worked a pink udder, grunting with the effort.

"If you run this place, you've got a customer," Fargo said in his broken border Spanish, lifting his voice above the wind.

"*Sí, sí,*" the man growled. With a grunt, he stood and walked around behind the cow—a short, loose-limbed man with long, gray hair, full beard, and an unlit corncob pipe in his mouth. He wore a striped serape over his loose woolen smock, and ambled over to Fargo, muttering Spanish curses.

Fargo swung down from the Ovaro and turned to face the barn as the liveryman approached. Ten feet away, the man stopped suddenly, sucking in a surprised breath. "Oh, forgive me. I did not realize—"

He cut himself off, scrutinizing Fargo with a heavy-browed frown.

Fargo held his gaze, staring down at the man who stood a good foot shorter. "Didn't realize what?" he said in English, then repeated it in Spanish.

The old man continued staring. A slow, bemused

smile dimpled his brick red cheeks and lifted his silver beard. "Senor, if you were not a *norteamericano*, I would think you were the brother of a local *Mejicano!*"

"I don't have any kin in this hellhole. At least, none that I know about." Fargo slung his saddlebags over his left shoulder, then slid his Henry repeater from its saddle sheath. "Take good care of this fella for me. Water, hay, half bucket of oats every day. Curry him good and tend his hooves. Back right frog tends to draw pebbles. I'll pay you when I leave."

He leveled a hard gaze on the shorter gent—the gaze of a saddle-owly border tough in bad need of a drink. "Any decent digs in town?"

The old Mexican caught the reins Fargo threw at him, wincing as they lightly slapped his face, and glanced at Fargo demurely—well accustomed to truckling to pistoleros, no doubt. And pistoleras.

"*Sí, Senor.* The Rio Grande. Big white adobe just down the street. But you won't get a room there. The gang of El Oso Loco and Senorita Diablo has taken it over." The liveryman rubbed his hand on his vest pensively, and a cunning light entered his eyes. "You might try my sister's place, Doña Flora's, just up the block. Her name is in big blue letters over the door. She boils the bedding once a week, serves the best *menudo* in the country, and has a couple of plump whores who will do anything you want." He grinned, biting down on his pipe. *"Como no, Senor?"* What more is there?

"Gracias," Fargo said. In town only three minutes, and he already knew where the gang was holed up. Maybe this was going to be easier than he'd thought. . . . "I'll have a drink and a look around."

As he hefted his saddlebags and rifle, he patted the pinto's rump and headed for the open doors, the hinges of which squawked in the gusting wind.

Behind him, the liveryman said, "If it's drink you're looking for, Doña Flora makes the best *baconora*—"

"Yeah, I know," Fargo said as he moved through the doorway and into the deserted street. "Best *baconora* in the country . . ."

"Cheap, too!" the old man intoned behind him, the wind nearly drowning his words.

The Trailsman tramped north along the street, keeping to the west side. He'd seen the big adobe hotel when he'd glassed the town from the hill, on the plaza and near the cathedral. As he moved past the dry fountain in the middle of the plaza, he scrutinized the hotel again now—easily the biggest building in town.

It was an old, two-story, Spanish-style adobe with pillars and arches and narrow, wrought-iron balconies off the upper story windows. RIO GRANDE was painted in large black letters over the first-story arches fronting the broad front door. The wind splattered sand against it, and a tumbleweed rolled down the boardwalk under the arbor. Out of sight at the back, a loose shutter banged, the reports muffled by the storm.

With its windows shuttered against the wind, the hotel looked abandoned. It was probably far from that. The gang was likely snuggled down with free-flowing liquor and whores.

Were Deana and the boys being held there, as well?

He'd have to find a way into the place. And what better way than by invitation?

Fargo stopped and looked around the plaza from under his pulled-low hat brim, stepping to one side to avoid a blowing tin can. Directly across the plaza from the hotel sat a cantina—just a squat, cracked adobe with one window and a grass curtain for a door. The building had probably served many purposes over the years, but the word scratched over the door in coal now announced, simply and succinctly, TEQUILA.

Saddle on his shoulder, Fargo bulled through the curtain and stopped just inside the door. The place—long and narrow from front to back—was dark as a

111

cave, lit only by murky daylight pushing through cracks in the thick adobe walls and the loose-fitting shutter over the front window, and from around the front door curtain.

The elaborate mahogany bar ran along the right wall, with a dozen or so rickety tables on the left. Bullet holes pocked the adobe, and here and there was a brown smear of old blood.

One man stood at the bar, near the door. Leaning forward with elbows on the mahogany, he swiveled his head to peer back at Fargo over his shoulder. The barman—tall, wire-thin, with a thick wing of raven hair hanging over one eye, and a pencil-line mustache—stood behind the bar with a corncob in his hands, frozen in the act of shucking. A pile of husks lay on the bar, six or seven cobs stacked neatly beside it.

A man and a woman sat together in the room's rear shadows, the woman straddling the man's right knee, the top of her white dress pulled down to her waist. Another man sat at the same table as the couple, head in his arms, the steepled crown of his sombrero aimed at the girl's slender, brown back like a shotgun barrel. His gravelly snores resounded above the wind's screech and groan.

The other man and the girl had both turned to stare at Fargo. A cigarette drooped from the man's mustachioed lips, smoke curling toward the rafters.

Fargo glanced at the barman, who was staring at him dully. "Tequila."

He made his way to a table halfway down the room and plopped his saddlebags over a chair. He kicked another chair out, sat down with his back to the wall, and laid the Henry across the table before him. Leaning back with a sigh, he stretched his legs under the table and crossed his arms on his chest.

The wind whistled through a crack in the adobe above his head. The drunk man continued snoring into his arms. Fargo didn't turn his head, but he could feel the stares of the other man and the girl.

On the other side of the room, the tall barman filled a shot glass from a clear bottle, then walked around the end of the bar and set the tequila on the table before Fargo. Fargo flipped a couple of coins on the table. Leaning forward and swiping the coins with his right hand into the palm of his left, the barman cast a lingering glance at the Trailsman, then turned and strode back behind the bar.

He muttered something the Trailsman couldn't hear above the snoring and the wind. The man standing at the bar near the door cast another glance at Fargo over his shoulder, turned his head forward, then chuckled as he lifted a beer glass to his mouth.

Fargo looked to his left. The man and the girl were indeed staring at him, the girl half turned to reveal one firm, pear-shaped breast. The man was a round-faced little *maton* with a thin goatee and mustache, his felt sombrero tipped far back on his head. His brown eyes were glassy from drink.

Fargo lifted his shot glass and nodded at the hard-case and the girl. *"Salud!"*

He threw back the tequila—he'd tasted worse, but not by much—and set the glass on the table. He winced as he swallowed, the pungent brew burning his gut like liquid fire.

The Mexican growled at the girl, waving his hands impatiently. She frowned and scrambled off his knee as he gained his feet, bumping the table before him. He pushed past the *puta* to stand on the far side of his table. He took a deep breath, hiked his cartridge belt higher on his hips, adjusted the six-shooter and holster thonged low on his right thigh, and sauntered between tables, keeping his speculative, belligerent gaze locked on Fargo.

Fargo remained frozen in his chair, arms crossed on

113

13

Fargo poked his hat brim off his forehead and locked eyes with the round-faced bandito glaring down at him. He remembered Deana's scream, and the bloody bodies and burned wagons.

"I'm your worst fuckin' nightmare if you don't stop blockin' my view, *friend*," he growled under his breath. "There's little enough worth lookin' at in this town. I sure as hell don't wanna sit here, starin' at *you*."

The man who'd been sleeping chuckled softly. The apron and the other customer didn't make a sound.

The round-faced Mexican cast a hard glance at his partner. The man stopped chuckling. The whore stood beside him, staring warily at Fargo as she slid her dress straps up her arms, slowly covering her breasts.

Turning back to the Trailsman, the round-faced bandito leaned slowly forward, placing both hands flat on Fargo's table while shaping a slow smile with only his lips, spreading his black mustaches. "You know just the right thing to say, *amigo*"—he leaned on his left hand and reached for his Navy Colt with his right—"for a one-way ticket to *hell*!"

He hadn't closed his fingers around the revolver's bone grips, however, before Fargo shook his Arkansas toothpick out of his right sleeve and into his palm, raised it high, and slammed it down hard. The blade pierced the middle of the man's brown hand, driving between the V-shaped bones behind the middle knuckles, and into the table beneath it with a loud thud.

The round-faced bandito bellowed like a felled ox. Crouching over the table, face swollen, he slapped his right hand toward the knife protruding from his left, reconsidered, and reached again for his pistol. His eyes found Fargo as he jerked the revolver free of its holster.

Fargo had anticipated the move. His own Colt was already in his hand, cocked and aimed at the bandito's head. It didn't stop the man from bringing his pistol up.

The Trailsman cursed silently as he squeezed his Colt's trigger. *Ka-boom!*

In the close quarters, the report sounded like a cannon blast. Everyone jumped and the whore yelped as the bullet punched through the man's forehead, spraying blood, brains, and bone out the back of his head and across the table and chairs behind him.

The round-faced Mex's eyelids fluttered as his body slackened and hung toward the floor, suspended by his hand, still pinned to the table by the toothpick. The strain caused more dark blood to gush up from between the split knuckles.

Fargo glanced to his left, where the dead man's friend stood uncertainly and was reaching for his own holstered six-shooter. The Trailsman angled his revolver toward him, and clicked back the hammer. The bandito's hand froze on his holstered Remington's walnut grips.

He grinned, showing a cracked eyetooth beneath his scraggly mustache.

"Heee," he said slowly, raising both hands chest high, palms out.

He backed away from the table and, keeping his gaze locked with Fargo's, sidestepped toward the front door curtain. His Chihuahua spurs chinged softly. Before the curtain, he stopped, stared at Fargo, then lowered his hands, turned, and pushed outside.

The man at the bar now stood sideways to it, half facing Fargo, staring at the dead man. The barman sighed, picked up another ear of corn, and began shucking it. The whore swallowed hard, then turned, crossed herself, and hurried into the room's rear shadows.

Somewhere back there, a door closed loudly and a bolt was thrown.

The Trailsman holstered his .44, then reached forward and yanked his Arkansas toothpick out of the table. The man's hand slipped off the table and followed the rest of his body to the floor. There was a heavy thump and slap.

"*Es el dia!*" muttered the man standing on Fargo's side of the bar. He turned around and asked the barman for another tequila.

As the barman refilled his customer's shot glass, Fargo raised his own glass and said he'd have another one, as well. He kept his voice mild, offhand, but his guts were strung tight as piano wire.

He hadn't intended on pushing as hard as he had. He'd known he might have to kill one of the gang to get the rest of the gang's attention, but the way he'd done it might rub the others the wrong way.

One thing was for certain—he'd know in short order what their exact responses would be.

"If I were you, Senor," said the barman as he held the bottle over the Trailsman's shot glass, refilling it, "I'd prance out of here like a chaparral cock, and never ride south of the border again. But then, it is no doubt too late for running."

"I reckon it depends on where I choose to take it— from the front or the back." Fargo threw back the shot, wincing at the burn. "Better leave the bottle."

* * *

Waiting for the bandits, the Trailsman refilled his revolver's empty chamber, wiped his toothpick off on the dead bandit, then had another shot of tequila.

Outside, the wind blew, pelting the adobe with sand. There was the muffled clatter of a shutter banging its frame.

The barman continued shucking his corn. When he had only one ear left, the vaquero leaning on the bar straightened suddenly and turned to the curtained doorway. He edged the curtain aside, peeked through the crack, then moved back to the bar and threw down the last of his tequila.

"I think I will brave the windstorm, and head back to my estancia," he told the barman in Spanish. Donning his straw sombrero, he glanced at Fargo. "*Hasta la vista, Senor.* I pray a peaceful home awaits you with the saints."

He crossed himself, steadied his feet beneath him, and ambled into the shadows at the back of the room. He'd no sooner disappeared than the *ching* of large-roweled spurs rose outside amidst the howling wind and ticking sand.

The grass curtain was thrown aside and a big, bearded man strode into the tavern. He was well over six feet tall and had features so similar to Fargo's that the Trailsman felt as though he were seeing himself in a mirror, except that El Oso Loco's brown eyes were set deep beneath a heavy brow. One was pearl-colored and dead. The other owned the cold, sneering cast of the savage border thug.

He was followed by a half-dozen other men in serapes or calico shirts and wearing sombreros, fringed chaps, or bell-bottom breeches and six-shooters. They swaggered in, blinking the sand from their eyes and beating it off their hats as El Oso Loco walked along the bar, canting his head from side to side and crouching to see under Fargo's hat brim.

He stopped before the bar and stared at Fargo hard.

He wasn't wearing a hat, and his long, wavy black hair was flecked with sand. He wore a black shirt and fringed bullhide chaps over white slacks adorned with silver conchos, and his revolver was thonged low on his right thigh, while a pepperbox jutted from a cross-draw rig high on his left hip.

"*Mi amigo,* Rocco, tells me a man who looks *just* like me killed my other friend, Pancho Corona." El Oso Loco dropped his gaze to the dead man on the floor for the first time. He raised his good eye again to Fargo, and clucked, wrinkling the seamed brown flesh over the bridge of his nose. "Senor, we better be brothers or half brothers or *some*thing, or I am going to have take revenge on behalf of my good friend, Pancho."

Fargo sat his chair, one hand wrapped around his half-empty shot glass, the other around the bottle. "Your friend Pancho was trying to feed me a pill I couldn't digest. If you take offense to a man trying to defend himself, then let's get on with it."

As El Oso Loco flared his nostrils and dropped his hands straight down by his side, footsteps sounded beyond the cantina's grass curtain. The curtain was swept aside, and another bandito walked into the room, swaggering even more than the others.

"What is this I hear about some gringo who looks like El Oso Loco?"

Not a *bandito,* Fargo saw as the woman, dressed in tight denims and wearing a brown cartridge belt with two matched Allen and Wheelock .32s, pushed past the men lined up along the bar. A *bandita* with full hips, narrow waist, and high, pointed breasts thrusting beneath her black-and-white calico blouse, open to reveal a deep valley of golden cleavage. Her long, black hair was mussed and sandy, lying in wind-whipped swirls about her fine-boned cheeks and proud shoulders.

She moved into the room, her eyes quickly finding Fargo. The lustrous black orbs darted to the dead man on the floor, to Fargo, to El Oso Loco, then back to Fargo again. She stopped near El Oso Loco, crossed her arms on those magnificent breasts, and cocked a spurred boot heel. A cool, bemused smile tugged at her full, rich lips.

"Holy Christ, your long-lost brother, eh, you crazy bear? You didn't tell me you had a twin."

"This *yanqui* is no blood of mine."

"Blue eyes," Senorita Diablo observed, her smoky gaze riveted on the Trailsman. She reached over and rubbed El Oso Loco's slight paunch. "And he doesn't wear quite as much tallow, uh?"

El Oso Loco's right eyelid flickered as he continued glaring over the dead man at the Trailsman.

Fargo threw back the last of his tequila and raised the bottle. "Drink, Senorita?"

"Ah, the gentleman wants to buy a lady a drink." She glanced at El Oso Loco and moved toward Fargo's table, running her eyes across his chest and then back up to his face. "A couple of you boys haul out this human trash. The padre's hogs are hungry. Then pull your horns in and have a drink while I pinch the *yanqui* for tequila."

"Get away from there, *chiquita*!" El Oso Loco bellowed, chin tipped toward his chest, heavy brows hooding his eyes.

The senorita laughed as two of the other men quickly dragged the dead man toward the curtained doorway, eager to get out of the line of fire. Senorita Diablo canted her head toward El Oso Loco and said to Fargo, "Will you buy him one, too? He is—how do you say?—the jealous type."

The Trailsman glanced at the bartender standing against the back bar, looking pale. "Apron, two more glasses!"

"I order you to get away from there, *chiquita*. The gringo has an appointment with San Pedro!"

Keeping her back to the big man, the senorita

kicked a chair out from Fargo's table and plopped down, her hair bouncing on her shoulder. She dug a makings sack from the breast pocket of her blouse and tossed it on the table. "*Dios mio!* Stop being so dramatic, you crazy bear. The gringo's going nowhere in this storm, and he is one man against many. You have all night to kill him."

She leaned forward over her makings sack, shoving her ripe breasts over the table, where the Trailsman had a good look at her cleavage, and said huskily, "Any man who can turn Pancho into a bloody pulp on the floor deserves one last drink with a woman, no?"

The barman came out from the bar with two shot glasses in his hand, giving El Oso Loco a wary glance. He stepped into the line of fire between Fargo and the bandit leader long enough to plop the two glasses on the table between Fargo and Senorita Diablo, then bolted wide and sought refuge again behind the bar.

Keeping one eye on El Oso Loco and one eye on the man's woman—a real heart-stopper who, given her transgressions against the Trailsman, wasn't going to be hard to kill—Fargo splashed tequila into the two fresh glasses.

The knot in his stomach loosened when El Oso Loco relaxed his gunfighter's crouch and moseyed over to the table. He kicked out a chair to the right of Senorita Diablo, adjust his pistol on his hip, and sat down. Meanwhile, the other banditos turned to the bar and, murmuring amongst themselves, ordered drinks.

"Don't think we are friends because you buy us drinks, *yanqui*," said El Oso Loco, holding his shot glass between his crud-encrusted thumb and index finger. From the smell of his breath, he'd been drinking for a couple of days. "No man, especially a gringo, kills one of my men and lives to boast."

"One of *our* men, *mi amor*," corrected Senorita Diablo, her cool, coquettish eyes on Fargo. "Don't forget

121

that I was the one who brought Pancho into the group—*after* he killed Luis's nephew down in Rio Vista." She waved a hand to dismiss the issue and said to Fargo as she began building a cigarette, "What are you called, big gringo? And what brings you to La Escondida? Most strangers concerned for their health know to steer clear of this place."

"I reckon I'm too much of a stranger to have gotten the word," said Fargo, sitting negligently back in his chair, feigning a relaxed air. "What's so dangerous about this place? The wells tainted?"

Senorita Diablo smiled as she poked the cigarette between her delectable lips and struck a match on the table. She had the regal bearing of the father she'd maimed and disgraced.

Still holding his tequila glass on the table before him, and leaning pugnaciously forward, El Oso Loco said, "The lady asked who you were and what you're doing here, Senor. I suggest you answer."

Fargo glanced at the senorita. "Does he need his feed changed, or is he just naturally contrary?" He turned to El Oso Loco. "The name's Steve Farmer. Just passin' through to points south. Had a little trouble north of the border. I didn't come here intending to kill anybody, but your boy gave me no choice."

Senorita Diablo took a drag off her cigarette and blew the smoke over Fargo's head. Her eyes were glued to his. "He was a pistolero renowned throughout Sonora. The killer of many. You handled him rather well."

Fargo held her gaze. "Just lucky, I reckon."

"I do not believe in luck."

El Oso Loco had been shuttling his jealous gaze between the Trailsman and Senorita Diablo. "Enough talk, Senor Farmer!" he exploded. "You have killed a pistolero weakened from drink. I am sober as the pope. Suppose we go outside, and we see how your luck holds against me—a gunman renowned throughout northern Méjico!"

Holding her cigarette in one hand, that elbow resting on the table, Senorita Diablo refilled her tequila glass with the other. She shook her head. "Speaking as a woman, I'd rather see a test of *physical* strength."

El Oso Loco looked at her, frowning. She kept staring at Fargo. "I challenge you, Senor Farmer, to an arm-wrestling match against my crazy bear. What do you say?"

Fargo shuttled his glance back and forth between them, and hiked a shoulder. "What's in it for me?"

"Your life," she said, blowing another smoke plume. "And *me*."

El Oso Loco jerked his head toward her, his face turning sunset red beneath his natural brown, the ruined eye glowing as though backlit. *"Fucking* puta *bitch!"*

He started out of his seat, balling his fists, but froze suddenly. In her left hand, Senorita Diablo clicked back the hammer of the .32 revolver she had snugged against El Oso Loco's right ear. She laughed with delight. "No, you crazy, jackal. You are going to fight *him*, not me. And, if you do not win, it will be a cold day in hell before you frolic between *my* legs again!"

14

Senorita Diablo smashed the necks off of a couple of empty tequila bottles and set the broken shards on the table at which the Trailsman and El Oso Loco sat in the middle of the room, glaring at each other.

The gang members gathered around in hushed silence, as did the tall barman, keeping to the group's periphery, an expectant but cautious cast to his gaze. The senorita placed both her hands over the tops of Fargo's and El Oso Loco's, their grips so tight their knuckles turned white. On the table to each side, the glass shards winked in the wan gray light angling through the wall cracks.

"Begin!"

The senorita removed her hands from the opponents' fists and both men's chairs creaked under the strain of their flexing bodies.

The Trailsman had arm-wrestled often before—it was a favorite pastime of the pioneers he guided, one in which they indulged while sitting around campfires long after supper and after the last woman and child had retired to their bedrolls.

Obviously, El Oso Loco was an old hand at the sport, as well, and he was as similar in strength to Fargo as he was in appearance. Their entwined fists barely moved more than an inch or two in either direction. Their knuckles bulged and turned white, their thumbs shifting slightly, their fingernails pink with expanding blood vessels. Their chairs creaked and groaned.

Senorita Diablo sat on a nearby table edge, her boots on a chair, a half-empty tequila bottle in one hand, a cigarillo in the other. Fargo felt her smug, bemused gaze moving between him and her beau.

Around her, the banditos smoked and drank and watched in heavy silence. Like the senorita—probably following her example, in fact—they remained silent. There was no cheering. They obviously feared the woman. Like Fargo himself, they probably weren't sure which man she was pulling for, if either.

Outside, the wind howled, pointing up the heavy silence inside the tavern.

About seven minutes into the game, Fargo felt El Oso Loco's liquor consumption begin to take its toll. The man's hand grew mushy and he was breathing harder, though his grisly, one-eyed glare did not leave Fargo's eyes as the Trailsman began to edge the man's knuckles slowly toward the glass shards.

He pulled back slightly. Should he go ahead and whip this son of a bitch; grind his knuckles into the glass? Or should he let El Oso Loco win?

He glanced at the senorita, whose eyes narrowed slightly at his gaze before she slipped the cigarillo between her lips.

Of course, he might still have to parry El Oso Loco's wrath, but there was a chance El Oso Loco, being as macho a border *maton* as Fargo had ever known, would honor the terms of the fight. If he didn't, he might lose face with his men. . . .

Fargo tightened his jaws and flexed his forearms until the muscles and sinews stood out in sharp relief, large as fence posts beneath his rolled sleeve. With a low grunt, he fought El Oso Loco's broad fist down, down, down toward the jutting shards.

"Bastardo!" the bandito leader raked out, his bearded cheeks balled with rage and horror.

He fell silent as Fargo rammed the back of his hand into the glass. Around him the banditos sucked air through their teeth or groaned, chairs squawking as a few rose for a better look. Senorita Diablo smiled at the pebblelike grinding of the glass beneath El Oso Loco's fist, the blood running out from his torn knuckles.

El Oso Loco shook slightly and bowed his head over his hand, cheeks dimpling where his jaws hinged. The jaws tightened more as Fargo gave the knuckles an extra turn from side to side. One of the large shards cracked with a soft ping.

"Unnh . . ." said El Oso Loco softly, turning his head slowly from side to side and opening his fingers. He kept the back of his hand flat against the table.

Fargo pulled his own hand away.

El Oso Loco's wince became a smile as the man lifted his head. His liquid brown eye, the white slightly red, bore into Fargo's. The pearl one glowed behind the fluttering lid.

"Oooooohhhh," said one of the men behind the senorita.

The Trailsman sat straight in his chair, arranging a casual expression as he flexed his fist. "Don't feel too bad," he said in his cow-pen Spanish. "The glass on my side looked a might sharper."

El Oso Loco bunched his lips as he lifted his hand. He turned it palm down and removed a couple of the largest shards, blood welling and dripping onto the table.

He glanced at Senorita Diablo. Apparently, the man didn't like the look in the woman's eyes.

He turned back to Fargo, stared at him hard, letting the blood drip freely from his hand to the table. In a blur of motion, he bolted out of his chair and snapped his bloody hand toward his right hip.

"Greet el diablo for me, gringo!"

El Oso Loco raised his Colt above the table, but before he could thumb back the hammer, Senorita Diablo jumped down from her perch and swung her half-empty tequila bottle by its neck in a downward-slicing arc. The bottle shattered against the back of the man's head, spraying tequila and jerking his head and shoulders to one side.

The pistol sagged in El Oso Loco's hand, then fell to the floor. The man's eyelids fluttered as he sagged heavily to his left before hitting the worn puncheons, chair and all, with a thunderous boom.

El Oso Loco sighed and lay still, half seated in his overturned chair. Blood welled from his head now as well as from his hand.

Silence.

Holding his Colt straight out in his right hand, Fargo looked around.

The half dozen banditos stood in a semicircle around him, staring down at their fallen *compañero*. Their bodies were tense, jaws rigid. Several had their hands on their holstered revolvers.

Senorita Diablo dropped what remained of her bottle and turned toward the gang members. The barman, standing behind them, leaped instinctively straight back, as though from a bounding lioness.

"You men tend his wounds and lay him out on a couple of tables. If he wakes up before morning, keep him here." She turned to give Fargo a coquettish look over her right shoulder, her thick, black hair winging out from her neck.

"What are you waiting for?" she asked. "Come on—I'll show you around."

She smiled and, rolling her hips seductively, moseyed toward the door. Fargo watched her push through the curtain with flair and disappear.

Slowly, he gained his feet. The banditos watched him, sneering, as he grabbed his rifle and saddlebags and, holding his pistol in his right hand but aiming it at the floor, sauntered toward the buffeting grass curtain.

It hadn't been easy, and he could just as easily be dead as still breathing, but it looked like he'd found a way into the hotel, where Deana and the boys were no doubt being held.

Halfway to the curtain, he turned around, then backed the rest of the way to the entrance. He ticked his hat brim at the banditos, still glaring at him over the slumbering heap of El Oso Loco, then holstered his pistol and pushed outside.

He stopped to one side of the door. It had grown grayer, the wind still shepherding tumbleweeds and dust along the street. Above the wind rose a woman's high-pitched laugh somewhere off to Fargo's right— no doubt a *puta* being entertained by one of the senorita's other gang members.

On the other side of the square's central fountain, and veiled by blowing dust, Senorita Diablo mounted the porch of the Spanish-style hotel. She melded with the shadows beneath the porch roof and pushed through the batwing doors. The Trailsman tipped his hat brim low and, shouldering the saddlebags and hefting the Henry, tramped across the square, swerving wide of the fountain.

He mounted the porch, spurs ringing on the flagstone steps, and peered over the batwings. Inside and down three steps sprawled a vast, cavernous saloon under an arched adobe ceiling adorned with wrought-iron chandeliers from which dust-laced cobwebs clung. None of the wall-mounted lanterns were lit, so Fargo couldn't see much even after he'd entered and descended the three steps.

Dark faces peered at him from the tables scattered around the room and from the bar on the far left. The air was heavy with the stench of sweat, alcohol, chili peppers, and the sweet perfume preferred by Mexican whores.

Following the *ching* of spurs on stone, growing fainter by the second, Fargo crossed the saloon floor, weaving around adobe pillars, and climbed a broad, stone staircase at the back. In the darkness of the balcony above, a shadow moved in time with the chinging spurs.

He followed the ringing until, moving down a broad hall with the ringing of his own spurs echoing loudly, he saw a slender woman's shadow stop before a door. There was the soft clink of a key in a lock. The door opened with a bark of rusty hinges, and the shadow disappeared.

Fargo approached the door and slowed. From the open doorway, he stood staring into the room. The senorita had removed her gun belt and thrown it over a chair back. Now she was kicking out of her boots, one hand on a bedpost.

In guttural Spanish, she said, "You'd have to have a pretty long cock to fuck me from there."

She laughed and gave a grunt as her right boot came off and hit the floor with a thud.

The Trailsman stepped into the room and kicked the door shut behind him. He dropped his left shoulder, let the saddlebags fall to a chair by the door, and then leaned the rifle against the wall.

"You get right to it."

Senorita Diablo unbuttoned her denims, pulled her shirttails out, and began unbuttoning her blouse. "I see no reason for ceremony."

As beautiful as the woman was, the Trailsman would rather have strangled her than make love to her, but he wouldn't learn where Deana and the Haggelthorpe boys were held from a corpse.

Reluctantly, he removed his cartridge belt and draped it over his saddlebags. As he kicked out of his boots, Senorita Diablo shucked out of her blouse, then lifted the chemise over her head, her thick black tresses spilling about her shoulders as she tossed the undershirt onto the floor.

Her high breasts jerked and swayed as she sat on the bed and wrestled out of the denims.

Naked, Fargo tossed his underwear in a corner with his buckskins, then turned back to the bed, and froze. Senorita Diablo stood before him in all her naked, brown-skinned, heavy-breasted glory, pink nipples jutting through the tattered curtain of her hair. Rising up on her toes, she snaked her arms around his neck and kissed him hungrily, groaning, probing his mouth with her tongue.

Her nipples raked his chest and, in spite of himself, he felt a prickling in his loins. He ran his hands up her slender back, beneath her hair, and felt his hardening member rub against the silken mat between her legs. He slid his hands down across her flaring hips to the full, smooth buttocks.

She sighed and, kissing him, took his member in both hands. It grew harder. She smiled, then knelt slowly before him and closed her mouth over his shaft. His blood rose at the wet warmth of her mouth and her lapping tongue, and the room spun.

Rising, she crawled onto the bed and lay on her back, staring at his erection and groaning with desire. "Come," she whined, shaking her hair out across her shoulders, grinding her heels into the mattress. "Get over here, gringo! I got a job for you, huh? You do it right, I might let you kill El Oso Loco in the morning!"

"You think so, do you?" Fargo grunted, and curled his upper lip as he crawled onto the bed and lowered himself between her spread knees. "Maybe I'll just finish him off tonight."

She laughed and ran her hands through his hair, nibbling his ears and wrapping her legs around his back. Her tequila-laced breath was hot in his face, her voice a raspy growl. "Maybe I will help you, huh? Not that you would need it, you big ornery *bastard*!"

As Fargo thrust his hips forward, his member sliding through her hot, wet portal, she dug her fingernails into his back, shrieking, "Uhhhhh . . . *fuck* me, gringo!" and closed her mouth over his shoulder, her teeth stabbing his skin until she nearly brought tears to his eyes.

The bed squawked and thumped as he rode her, thrusting hard. The senorita thrashed beneath him, gouging her heels into his sides, her fingernails digging into his shoulders, lips stretched back from her teeth.

It was like fucking a wild panther, and he was glad when he finally shot his seed. She apparently came at the same time, throwing her head as far back as she could, gripping the bars of the headboard, and keening like a tortured Apache witch.

She scissored her legs behind his back and held him there as she lay with her eyes squeezed shut, wincing and shuddering. "Oooh," she said when she opened her eyes, running her hands across his chest, squeezing his biceps, and caressing his legs with her feet. *"Tu muy hombre, gringo. Muy hombre!"*

"Glad ya enjoyed it."

"Don't speak in the past tense." She lifted her head and pounded his chest with the ends of her fists until he rolled over on his back. "We just got started!"

Grunting and sighing, she scrambled onto her knees, then straddled him, leaning down so that her hair brushed his chest. He took the heavy, dark globes of her breasts in his hands and kneaded them, fingering the large nipples, working him and her both into another frenzy.

She rose up slightly on her knees, positioned him beneath her, then impaled herself with a yelp.

He winced at the nerves rippling deep within his loins.

Dropping her head toward his chest so she could watch the workings between them, she lifted slowly on her haunches, then sank back down. She held there, pivoting off her hips as she ground her pelvis against his, then rose up again gradually. She repeated the procedure, increasing the pace until she was bouncing up and down on top of him in a preternatural hysteria, until she had the bed pitching like a mustang bronco with a grizzly in the barn.

Amidst the violent cacophony, the window shutter came loose from its latch and thudded against the frame. The water bowl rang. A lamp chimney tinkled, the guttering flame shunting shadows. A mirror slipped off its nail and crashed to the floor, and a water glass tumbled off the washstand a half second later.

Meanwhile, the senorita shrieked, groaned, yammered, and keened for a good ten minutes before she and the Trailsman exploded once more together—a long, bittersweet plunge into pure ecstasy.

Afterward, she fell straight back between her own heels and Fargo's legs.

She loosed a long, luxurious sigh.

The bedsprings gave a final squawk.

Except for his and the senorita's own labored breathing, silence. Fargo lay back against the sweat-damp pillow, feeling as though he'd just been pummeled by a whole covey of Sioux squaws armed with stone clubs.

He squeezed his eyes closed and tried to shake off the delirium. Now that he'd softened the bitch up—if there was such a thing—maybe he could find out about the hostages. . . .

He felt her push back to a kneeling position on top of him, her wet bush pushing down on his belly. Not again, he thought.

She leaned out over the edge of the bed, and there was a soft snapping sound, like the snap of a keeper thong released from a gun hammer.

He snapped his eyes open.

Too late.

She crouched over him, still straddling him, ramming the barrel of a cocked pistol against the underside of his chin.

She smiled. "Thought you'd fooled me, huh, Senor Fargo?"

15

As the cold, round pistol barrel bit into his chin, Fargo opened his mouth to respond with a question of his own, but stopped when someone tapped on the door.

Staring down at him angrily, the senorita said, "Who the hell is it?"

Someone cleared his throat. "It is Martinez, Senorita. I have food for the gringa."

The senorita kept her pistol barrel snugged against Fargo's chin. "Do you have a key?" she yelled at the door without moving her head.

"*Sí.*"

"Use it and leave me the hell alone."

"*Sí, sí, Senorita!*"

As he stared up at the senorita's beautiful, cunning eyes boring down at him, Fargo heard a key clink in a lock directly across the hall. Was Deana that close?

At the moment, she could have been three feet away for all the good it did him with the senorita's cocked pistol in his face.

He let out a long breath and lifted his chin slightly away from the gun barrel. "You were on the riverboat?"

"*Sí.*" Senorita Diablo shifted her hips, pressing her crotch against his belly and squeezing her knees against his sides. Her breasts, across which strands of black hair fell, jiggled and bounced. "How could I forget the *hombre grande* who swam to the boat with a girl on his arm and with gringos shooting at him from shore, then sent four men to Heaven with only a stiletto?"

Fargo sighed. Stupid not to have considered the possibility that she might have been the daughter the don had taken on the riverboat cruise, or that she might remember him.

"I always wondered how it would feel . . . a man like you thrusting between my legs. I must admit, El Oso Loco is no match for you . . . in more ways than one." The senorita scooted up higher on his belly and turned the pistol from left to right, keeping the barrel snugged against his chin. "What are you doing here, Trailsman? If it is the gringa and the skinny white boys you're after, I must apologize. You can't have them. They will bring good money from the miners in St. August—"

Knowing he was at the end of his rope, Fargo decided to take a chance. He thrust his left hand up quickly, swiping the backside of it against the underside of the senorita's wrist. The gun popped, drilling a bullet into the adobe wall above Fargo's head.

The senorita grunted sharply and tried to bring the gun back down, but the Trailsman grabbed her wrist and squeezed. She screamed as her fingers opened and the revolver dropped to the bed. Fargo stifled the scream by smashing his right fist across the senorita's left cheek.

She flew sideways, hit the bed on her back and, after the bed stopped bouncing, lay still, one leg curled beneath her. She was out like a blown lamp, eyes closed, lips parted slightly. Blood glistened along a two-inch length of split skin on the nub of her left cheekbone.

Fargo plucked the gun from the bed and swung his legs to the floor. He froze, pricking his ears.

No sounds but the wind outside and the soft complaints of the bedsprings as he breathed. The banditos were either so accustomed to pistol shots that they didn't react to them anymore, or they were too drunk to hear.

Fargo gained his feet and looked around the room, his eyes darting to the washbowl and pitcher, and the top of the oak dresser, before he found a key peeking out from beneath the guttering lamp. He hoped it was the right one.

When he'd dressed and draped his saddlebags over his shoulder, he hefted the Henry and walked to the door. He stopped with one hand on the knob and glanced back at the bed.

The senorita lay sprawled on her back, her heavy, round breasts half covered by her hair. She hadn't moved. She wasn't dead; Fargo had heard her breathing.

He began to reach for his Arkansas toothpick, but stopped. Her own father wanted her dead, but Fargo couldn't do it. He'd probably live to regret it, but he couldn't do it.

He walked over to the bed, set down his rifle and saddlebags, then ripped up a sheet. He used one torn length to tie the senorita's hands behind her back. He gagged her with the other, tying the cloth tightly behind her head. Her eyelids fluttered and she gurgled, but otherwise didn't stir.

When that task was done, he emptied the senorita's guns, tossed her knife under the bed, then quietly slipped out of the room, palming the key he'd found under the lamp in his right hand.

In the semidark hall that smelled of old whiskey, candles, dust, and full slop buckets, he set his saddlebags on the floor, then pressed his ear to the door directly across from the senorita's.

Silence.

He poked the key in the lock and turned it slowly, wincing when it clicked—both relieved that the key worked and hoping like hell he'd found the right room.

He turned the knob, shoved the door open a foot, and poked his head inside. Two candles burned on a dresser. Between the dresser and the unmade bed on which a plate of food sat untouched, a slender figure sat slumped on the floor, silhouetted by the candlelight.

Fargo stepped into the room and eased the door shut behind him. He whispered, "Deana?"

The head came up suddenly, gold-blond hair catching the candlelight. There was a sharp intake of breath. "Skye?"

"Shhh!" He dropped to one knee before her, and she threw herself into his arms.

He could feel her heart beating. "How did you find me?" she whispered.

"Had a few lucky turns." Fargo placed his hands on her slender shoulders and held her away from him, his eyes boring into hers. "Where are the Haggelthorpe boys?"

"In a stable behind the hotel."

She wore only pantaloons and a thin chemise. "Get dressed fast. We're getting the hell out of here."

He straightened, pulled her to her feet, then strode to the door and cracked it. The hall was dark. He closed the door and turned to his right. Deana stood before him; she'd thrown on a red-and-white calico blouse and the skirt she'd been wearing when he'd last seen her.

Her took her by the hand, opened the door, and led her into the hall. When he'd closed the door and locked it, he picked up his saddlebags, switched his rifle to his left hand, and led Deana with his right, in the opposite direction from which he and Senorita Diablo had come. He couldn't cross the saloon, no doubt packed with bandits this time of the night, with the girl.

After ten minutes of stumbling around in the dark halls, hearing drunken snores, laughter, love grunts, and soft guitar music emanating from behind closed doors, he found a door that appeared to lead outside. He tripped the latch, threw the door wide, and looked around.

Stone steps dropped to the dark yard below. The wind had died. Fifty yards away and to the left, the cathedral loomed against the sky, its stout wooden cross silhouetted against twinkling stars.

Squeezing Deana's hand in his, Fargo started down the sand-dusted staircase, dropping onto the balls of his boots, his spurs ringing softly when they grazed a riser.

Below and to his right, someone cleared his throat and sniffed. Boots thudded on the hard-packed dirt.

Fargo stopped, and Deana gasped.

The footfalls grew louder. A shadow moved in the yard below and right of the stairs.

Fargo turned and ushered the girl back up the steps. Inside the hotel, he turned to close the door, but it was too late. The man—big, broad, and holding a rifle over his right shoulder—was already climbing the stairs heavily, breathing hard, a cigarette glowing beneath the brim of his black sombrero. The bandoliers crossed on his chest winked in the starlight.

Fargo left the door wide and pulled Deana back into the hall's heavy shadows, tinged with tobacco smoke and tequila. He stopped, shoved the girl down against the wall, dropped his saddlebags and rifle, then reached into his right boot for his toothpick. Palming the hide-wrapped handle, he straightened and pressed his back against the wall, trying to meld with the dark adobe.

The big man appeared in the doorway, nearly filling it, silhouetted against the night that was suddenly eerily still except for crickets chirping. The bandito's breath wheezed up from his chest, shoulders rising and falling sharply. He took a deep breath, took one step forward, and stopped.

"Who's there?" he said in Spanish.

As he began to lower his rifle from his shoulder, the Trailsman lurched forward and buried the toothpick's razor-sharp blade in the man's belly, stepping into the big body and thrusting up toward the heart.

The man grunted heavily, dropping his rifle and doubling over. *"Awwwwohhhh!"*

When Fargo felt the tip of his blade rend the tough heart muscle, he pulled it out, hot blood spewing after the blade. As the man dropped to his knees, clutching his bloody guts, Fargo quickly cleaned his toothpick and hand on the man's serape, replaced the blade in his boot, then picked up his saddlebags and rifle, and grabbed Deana's hand.

She rose reluctantly, taken aback by the killing. "Come on!" the Trailsman rasped, and headed down the stone steps, jerking the girl along behind.

At the bottom of the steps he turned and headed into the shadows at the rear of the hotel. An adobe stable shone in the starlight. It had a dilapidated lean-to and a corral in which weeds had grown up and tumbleweeds collected. The stable was large enough to house only three or four horses at a time, but it obviously hadn't been used in years—at least, not for stabling horses.

Fargo released Deana's hand and, looking around but seeing no one else in the alley, walked up to the two small doors that had been secured with a two-by-four plank shoved through their iron handles. The adobe on both sides was cracked and water-stained, and weeds grew tall along the stone foundation.

Fargo tapped on the door and said, just above a whisper, "Boys?"

Beyond the door there was a scuffing sound. Someone whispered too softly for Fargo to make out the words. Footsteps grew, and the voice of the older Haggelthorpe boy, Jim, said, "Mr. Fargo?"

Fargo removed the board from the door handles and pulled the right door open. Jim Haggelthorpe stood before him, tall and lanky, with a shock of wheat-colored hair hanging over his forehead. He squinted sleepily. His right eye was swollen, his cracked lips scabbed.

He smiled with disbelief. "How in the hell did you find us?"

The younger, shorter Peter materialized from the shadows behind him. His lower lip trembled. "M-Mr. Fargo . . . ?" His blond hair, even lighter than his brother's, looked like a tumbleweed tangled about his head.

Fargo held a hand up as he glanced around the alley. Turning back to the boys, he said softly, "You two fit to travel?"

"I'll say we are!" said Jim through a relieved sigh.

"Follow me," Fargo said. "We're gonna move fast, but as quiet as Apaches. Can you do that?"

The boys nodded eagerly.

Probably because most of the banditos were in drunken stupors or passed out altogether, it was relatively easy getting Deana and the Haggelthorpe boys out of the alley, across the village's cobbled main street, and into the livery barn.

The liveryman wanted nothing to do with rigging their horses, and locked himself in his tack room, but Fargo, Deana, and the boys quickly saddled their own mounts—the Ovaro and three of the gang's best-looking Arabs, actually—and led them to the barn's rear doors.

Shoving one door open, Fargo looked around the alley behind the stable. All was dark and quiet, with only a couple of coyotes yammering in the hills rising before him.

Fargo ordered the others to mount up, then swung into his own saddle, looking around again, getting his bearings, relieved to feel the magnificent stallion beneath him once more.

Now, if they could head straight west and skirt the town before gaining the trail . . .

A girl's shout raised the hair on the back of his neck. "Where do you think you are going, Senor Fargo?"

He jerked his head toward the corner of the stable. Senorita Diablo rose from behind a rain barrel, holding a Colt revolving rifle negligently over her right shoulder. Fargo reached for his pistol.

He hadn't gotten the gun halfway out of the holster before a gun flashed and boomed on the opposite side of the open stable doors. The bullet burned a furrow across Fargo's right cheek, knocking him sideways. As the Ovaro spooked, Fargo was jolted toward the opposite side of his saddle.

A second later, he hit the ground on his back.

"Uff!"

"Why do you run with your tail between your legs?" shouted El Oso Loco in Spanish. "Our fight is *far* from over!"

As the Ovaro skitter-stepped sideways, Fargo looked up. The big man, a white bandage wrapped around the top of his head, staggered toward him, his bulky frame silhouetted against the sky.

Starlight winked off the big Dragoon aimed straight out from his right shoulder.

16

Fargo cursed savagely and ducked his head as El Oso Loco's heavy Colt flashed and boomed once more. The ball sizzled past the Trailsman's left ear and into a rock behind him. Deana and the boys' mounts all screamed at the shot and increased their bucking, nearly throwing Peter from his saddle.

"Skye!" Deana screamed.

El Oso Loco continued stalking toward Fargo, cocking his pistol. Fargo threw himself sideways as the Dragoon exploded. Fargo hit the ground, rolled off his right shoulder, bolted off his heels, and dove forward.

He slammed his head into El Oso Loco's belly.

The big bandito went over backward, his gun arm slamming down on Fargo's left shoulder, the pistol slinging another slug skyward. Fargo fell on top of the man, pushing up on his outstretched arms.

"Ride!" he shouted to Deana and the boys, then delivered a savage right jab to El Oso Loco's cheek.

As hooves thundered and tack squawked, the Mexican grunted, squeezing his eyes shut. He lifted his head and began pulling his pistol down. Fargo punched him again, then grabbed his own .44 and fired from point-blank range.

The bandito yowled, his beard bunching, as the slug drilled through his belly.

Fargo squinted down his Colt's barrel. "This is for

the pilgrims you killed on the other side of the border, you son of a bitch!"

"*No!* Have mercy!"

Fargo fired two more shots into the same hole. "*Eyeeeeeeee!*" El Oso Loco screamed, kicking his legs wildly and tipping his head far back in the dust, blood oozing through his gritting teeth.

A rifle cracked behind Fargo.

"No!" Deana shouted.

A horse whinnied.

The Trailsman whipped around. Deana's horse was pitching in the shadows on the other side of the livery barn. There was a thud as a figure fell against a corral, and Senorita Diablo cursed loudly in Spanish. A second curse was clipped as Deana's dun pitched again with an enraged whinny.

Shouts and inquiring yells rose from the direction of the square.

Fargo pushed off his knees and ran to the Ovaro, side-stepping on the other side of the alley near a wood pile, its reins dangling. Fargo grabbed the reins, leaped into the saddle, and heeled the pinto toward Deana's bucking dun.

As he reached down and grabbed the dun's bridle, he saw Senorita Diablo lying facedown in the gap between the buildings, her rifle six feet beyond her. In the other end of the gap, shadows jostled. The other banditos had heard the gunfire and were heading this way.

The Trailsman got the dun turned and headed up the alley, toward the south end of town. "*Go!*" He fell back and slapped the dun's right hip, the report sounding like a pistol crack.

He glanced back at Senorita Diablo as the Ovaro tore off after the dun. Was she dead? He should have shot her when he'd had his second chance, but he'd hesitated, and it was too late now.

Shouts lifted behind him. A revolver cracked three times, the third slug plunking into a stone well house as Fargo swerved the Ovaro around a chicken coop, then leaned forward as the horse leaped a boulder. Ahead, Deana's head bobbed and swayed, hair flying out behind her, the galloping dun's shod heels flashing in the starlight.

Five minutes later, on the winding cart trail they'd followed as the path of least resistance, in the rocky hills southwest of the village, Deana's dun slowed. Fargo looked beyond her. In a crease between rocky hogbacks, two horseback riders sat slouched in their saddles.

"Which way, Mr. Fargo?" Jim shouted from atop El Oso Loco's Appaloosa.

Fargo checked down the pinto and stared back at the village—the silhouetted rooftops humped in the hollow below. He could hear the muffled thuds of galloping horses and the intermittent pops and booms of the banditos, enraged and shooting at shadows.

"We'll have to feel our way till we can shake the bandits off our trail," Fargo said. He turned to Deana, sitting her dun a few feet away, then looked at the boys. "Everybody all right?"

They all nodded.

Fargo swung the Ovaro forward and touched his spurs to its flanks. "Follow me, and stay close!"

Heading cross-country but angling north, Fargo led Deana and the Haggelthorpe boys through the dense chaparral limned by starlight before taking to the higher, pine-studded reaches. The Trailsman paused several times while the others pushed on, and heard the soft thuds of distant riders punctuated by occasional, outraged shouts.

It was near dawn when he paused again, atop a mountain shoulder, and stared out over the bench he and the others had just traversed. Ten or so purple shadows weaved and bobbed amongst the sage and creosote. The lead rider's long hair bounced across her shoulders while the cream-colored horse beneath her strode fluidly, tirelessly.

Senorita Diablo.

Fargo poked his hat brim off his forehead and spat. If that had been a man lying in the gap between the livery barn and the corral, she'd be snuggling with the snakes rather than fogging his trail. She was a damn good tracker—he'd give her that. And a hell of a task-mistress, to boot. She'd kept her gang hot on the Trailsman's heels.

And because Fargo couldn't push the boys and Deana as hard as Senorita Diablo was pushing her men, she was steadily gaining on him. . . .

Swinging the Ovaro around, he headed down a hill and overtook Deana and the boys. He led them on a zigzagging course through the lower mountain slopes, then along a dry, rocky riverbed for about two miles, before swinging back north.

Daylight found them plodding along a canyon floor, eroded pink walls rising on both sides, with mud swallows and hawks screeching in the rookery for breakfast.

Behind Fargo, a saddle squawked, and a heavy thud and a grunt sounded. He whipped a look behind. Young Peter had fallen off his horse and lay sobbing in the dust.

"Pete!" Jim Haggelthorpe cried as he slipped down from his own claybank and knelt beside his brother.

"Get him back on his horse!" Fargo raked out.

Deana rode up from behind and dismounted her dun. Kneeling on the other side of Peter, she glanced at Fargo. "Skye, he's done in. Isn't there somewhere we can hole up for a while, let him catch his breath?"

Fargo lifted his gaze along their back trail. About a mile behind, the banditos were snaking along a butte shoulder, the senorita still in the lead. As the gang dropped out of sight, Fargo turned to look ahead over the Ovaro's twitching ears.

He sat up straight in the saddle, scouring the distance with his blue-eyed gaze, sweat runneling the dust on his face, then dropped out of his saddle. He hunkered down beside Peter, who sat in the trail, his sweat-soaked blond hair sliding in the hot breeze.

"Peter, I know you're tired. But you have to get back on your horse, son." He grabbed the boy's right arm, pulled him to his feet, then lifted him back onto his saddle. "You can rest soon."

The Trailsman turned to Deana and Jim standing before him, both looking worn, sweaty, and dusty. "You see that ridge yonder?" He put his arm around Deana's shoulders as he pointed to a ridge of andosite looming in the northwest, atop a steep, pine-carpeted slope. "Head for it. There's a saddle to the left, though you can't see it from here."

On the other side of the saddle, the rocky terrain was ripped with canyons. Plenty of places to hide. It was their only chance.

Deana shaded her eyes as she stared up at him. "What're you going to do?"

"I'm gonna buy us some time. If I don't catch up to you by the end of the day, camp on the other side of the ridge, then continue heading north tomorrow. You should reach the border in four, five days."

Jim turned to him, his battered face sunburned. "You can't take them all, Mr. Fargo. I'll stay and help."

"I don't intend on taking them all." Fargo led Deana to her horse and helped her mount. "But I can take out their leader and cull their herd, maybe discourage the others from continuing after you three."

"Skye," Deana said, staring down at him beseechingly. "Stay with us."

Fargo turned Peter's horse by its bridle. The boy

146

sat slouched but scared enough to do as he'd been told. "Get moving—all of you. Like I said, just keep heading north."

When Jim had mounted up and led Deana and Peter down the thin ribbon of old Indian trail they'd been following through the scrub and boulders, Fargo swung onto the Ovaro. He galloped the horse back the way he'd come, cresting one rocky rise before starting up another, even higher, rockier saddle.

Halfway to the ridgetop, he swung down from the saddle, dropping the Ovaro's reins and shucking his Henry. He grabbed a box of .44 shells from his saddlebags, emptied the box into his pockets, then levered a fresh shell into the Henry's breech.

Leaving the pinto to forage on the short grass growing around the rocks, Fargo tramped up the hillside and sidled between boulders at the top, doffing his hat and keeping his head down. He found a deep, rocky nest high on the other side of the ridge.

Propping one boot on a shelf before him, he leaned back against a flat-sided boulder, in the shade from another boulder looming above, and snugged the butt of his rifle against his cartridge belt, waiting. . . .

On the other side of the next sun-blasted rise, dust rose. Gradually, hoof thuds sounded, growing louder, shod hooves ringing like cracked bells. The cream barb appeared atop the rise, then started down, Senorita Diablo sitting tall in the saddle, her Colt rifle resting across her thighs. The other riders crested the ridge behind her and followed her down.

Hunkering low in his stone bunker, Fargo lowered his rifle and aimed down the barrel. He drew a bead on the senorita's chest, let the bead float around on her calico blouse and black vest until she was at the bottom of the grade, within fifty yards.

The banditos were so close that the Trailsman could hear the horses snorting, the saddles squeaking, and the bridle chains jangling.

The senorita put the barb up the next hill, heading nearly straight toward Fargo. As he planted his sites between those lovely cones pushing out her shirt and vest, and squeezed the Henry's trigger, she stopped suddenly, jerking back on the barb's reins, whipping her head around as though sensing the ambush.

Ka-boom!

The Henry's report echoed around the rocky ridges. The rider flanking the senorita screamed suddenly as he jerked back in his saddle, blood spurting from his neck. His horse whinnied and pitched, and the wounded man flopped across his cantle like a rag doll.

The horse sunfished, throwing the man suddenly sideways. He hit the ground in a cloud of dust and rolled behind a boulder.

Several of the other horses whinnied and Spanish warnings flew up as the senorita ditched her own startled mount and dove behind a cactus. Fargo planted a bead on a mounted rider, fired, and watched the man fly off the back of his horse as blood and brains spewed from the back of his head.

The Trailsman fired and levered, fired and levered, one shot flying wild but three more hitting a shoulder, a belly, and a chest before the remaining six riders, shouting and clutching rifles and kicking up dust, took cover behind boulders or shrub thickets.

The horses milled and whinnied, reins dangling, then scattered, several heading back the way they'd come while two headed off down the hollow, buck-kicking.

Fargo ejected a spent shell and heard it clink in the rocks behind him. "Not bad shootin'," he grunted. "If I do say so for myself."

He gazed down the rocky grade. The senorita poked her head out from the barrel cactus she'd taken cover behind. Fargo aimed hastily and fired two shots, gritting his teeth as the senorita pulled her head back behind the cactus. The Trailsman's two slugs nipped

148

only sand and gravel, and chewed a few pulpy slivers off the cactus.

A second later, the woman bolted out from behind the cactus and dove behind a boulder ahead and left of it.

Fargo ejected another smoking shell. "Bitch."

The other bandits were shouting back and forth. One ran out from behind his boulder, heading for the one ahead of it, teeth showing white in his brown, black-bearded face. Fargo cheeked the Henry again; fired. The bandito bolted sideways, chaps flapping madly, dropping his Remington repeater and grabbing his left hip.

"Bastardo!" he shouted.

A high cackling sounded from behind the senorita's boulder. She poked an eye out from the side and shouted, "You have made Fuguero very unhappy, Senor Fargo. Enjoy the feeling. You are outnumbered!"

"Come and get me, you whore!" Fargo slid back behind his rock cover. Two shots echoed, both slugs barking into the stone before him, spraying his nest with shards.

He stretched a look down the hill. The senorita's rifle, snaking around the side of her boulder, belched smoke. Fargo jerked back as the .56 slug ricocheted off a corner of the boulder before him, then slammed into the one behind.

A couple of stone slivers bit through his shirt, feeling like beestings.

The senorita shouted orders to her men. Fargo couldn't hear clearly, but he knew that she was directing them to work around him, try to get above and behind him while she kept him pinned down from her position at the base of the slope. It was what he'd expected; it was what he'd have done in her shoes.

The important thing was that he was buying Deana and the boys time to get into those badlands on the other side of the high basalt ridge.

17

The senorita did her job well. Between her rifle and pistol shots, Fargo caught only fleeting glimpses of the other banditos making their way up the hill around him, hopscotching from boulder to boulder. The advantage the Trailsman had, however, was that Senorita Diablo's Colt revolving rifle held only five rounds, and that her .32-caliber pistols weren't accurate at this range.

When he'd counted seventeen shots, instead of reloading, she called for Fuguero to toss her his Remington rifle. If Fargo had a chance, this was it.

Bounding straight up and over the boulder before him, he leaped to a flat one below and to the right. Two shots rang out from either side and above. As he leaped into a crack between two halves of the same rock, he caught a glimpse of the two men who'd been working their way down from the ridge crest.

He jerked the Henry to his shoulder, aimed up the hill to his left, and fired. As that bandito doubled up and dropped his rifle, Fargo fired uphill and right, his slug punching a bandito wearing a straw sombrero and red sash back against the rocks and out of sight.

A slug shattered against a rock to his right, followed by the rifle report from downhill. Levering a fresh shell, Fargo jerked around, aimed quickly, and fired. His slug tore up dust just behind Senorita Diablo as she pulled her head back behind the boulder.

The way she flinched told him he'd grazed her.

150

More shots rocketed around him. In the corner of his right eye, he saw two men scrambling toward him from the west, one leaping boulders while another crabbed along the ground, plowing caliche with his rifle butt.

A spur chinged near the Trailsman. He turned left to see three more men descending on him at an angle from upslope, eager grins on their dusty, dark faces, one man's sombrero blowing down his back as he leaped a boulder.

Fargo was surrounded.

"Kill the son of a bitch!" the senorita screamed in Spanish from downslope, her voice shrill with pain.

Fargo swung around, looking ahead and behind. If he was about to become a meal for the *zopilotes*, he'd take one or two more banditos with him. . . .

Senorita Diablo screamed, "*Wait!*"

Squeezing his rifle in both hands, Fargo turned toward her. She'd risen from behind the boulder and, blood running down from her bullet-burned forehead, began moving up the slope, holding the Remington's butt against her cartridge belt.

She showed her teeth like a feral dog. "He is mine."

Fargo jerked his gaze to both sides, then straight down the hill at the senorita striding toward him. Her eyes pinned on him, she kept her chin dipped devilishly, swinging her hips like a well set-up *puta* walking into a cantina to start business for the night . . . except that she held her rifle over her right shoulder.

Fargo held his rifle across his chest. His heartbeat quickened. He'd just found his next target.

Come on, you bitch. Just keep walking. Let me put this one between those big, beautiful jugs. . . .

Her black hair fluttered in the breeze as she climbed the rise and leaped onto a boulder ten feet in front of Fargo. The other banditos had stopped about the same distance away from him, grinning, holding their rifles across their chests.

The senorita cocked one hip, planted her fist on the other. Her shirt was unbuttoned to her vest, and her golden cleavage yawned. "How 'bout one last kiss . . . for old times . . . ?"

Fargo held her gaze for stretched seconds. He began shaping a smile but stopped suddenly as he swung the Henry's barrel toward her heaving bosom, and squeezed the trigger.

Click!

Fargo's gut fell. The Henry was empty.

"Wait!" the senorita screamed as the men on both sides of Fargo jerked to life, aiming their rifles. They froze, sliding their frantic, befuddled gazes between the Trailsman and Senorita Diablo.

The senorita smiled, black eyes glinting wickedly. "I was counting your shots, Senor, as you, no doubt, were counting mine." She threw head back and laughed. "Now, then . . . that kiss . . . ?"

"I'd rather kiss a buzzard."

The senorita's face grew hard as stone. "You will have your wish." She dropped the Remington's barrel to her right hand.

He flinched, expecting a bullet in his own gut, as one of the men to his left screamed suddenly. A rifle report made its way down the ridge. The bandito clapped one hand to the back of his neck, staggered past Fargo, and fell in a prickly pear patch. A half second later, another bandito screamed, and then the rifle volleys echoed down the ridge like thunderclaps, men dropping around Fargo like tin cans off fence posts.

The Trailsman dropped to one knee, glancing up at the smoke puffing around the boulders just below the ridge, blood spraying around him like red paint, the banditos shrieking, twisting, and falling.

To his right, the senorita cursed and dropped behind a low boulder, aiming her rifle toward the ridge.

Holding his empty rifle in his left hand, Fargo

palmed his revolver, cocked it, and aimed at the senorita. "Hold it."

She turned her head toward him, eyes flashing. He held her gaze as the last of the banditos died loudly and the rifle fire dwindled to silence. Suddenly, she jerked her rifle around, bringing the barrel to bear on Fargo.

The Colt cracked, powder smoke wafting. The senorita gave a clipped groan as the bullet tore through her chest and punched her back into the rocks and brush. She jerked for a moment, then lay still, sightless eyes staring up at the sky.

The Trailsman was staring down at the senorita when a Spanish-accented voice dropped from the ridge. "All clear, Senor?"

It was Don de la Garza's *segundo*, Fernando Sandoval.

Fargo straightened and glanced up the ridge, where five men in serapes and sombreros stared down at him, serapes and hat brims buffeting in the breeze. Sandoval and the don's vaqueros. Smoke wafted like fog along the ridgeline.

"All clear," Fargo called.

The men started down the ridge. Fargo sat on a boulder near the dead senorita. He was shaping a cigarette from his makings sack when Sandoval stepped onto the rock just above him and canted his gaze at the don's daughter. The *segundo* clucked, sighed, and scrubbed sweat from his shaggy brows with a shirtsleeve.

He turned to Fargo. "We were riding with the don to check the water holes," he said in a strange mix of Spanish and broken English. "We encountered the girl and the two boys. Lucky we did, eh, Senor?" Sandoval chuckled, but clucked sadly when he returned his gaze to Senorita Diablo, crossing himself.

"You got that right," Fargo said, lighting a lucifer on his thumbnail. "Much obliged."

"We sent the girl and the two boys on to the hacienda. They await you there." Sandoval paused. "I hate to say such an awful thing, Senor, but the don will be happy that you put down his daughter like the mangy bitch she was."

As Sandoval and the other vaqueros began going through the dead banditos' pockets, Fargo took a long drag off his cigarette and glanced up the ridge. The don stood atop a boulder near the crest, silhouetted against the sky. He wore a grand black-and-silver sombrero thonged beneath his chin, and his customary *charro* jacket and whipcord trousers, flared at the cuffs. His string tie fluttered up around his thin right shoulder.

"Come along, Senor Fargo," the don said, just loud enough for the Trailsman to hear. "The lobos are dead. The hunt is over. It is time for a drink, is it not?"

That night, after supper at the don's hacienda, Fargo and don de la Garza sat on the patio, smoking cigars and drinking cognac. The don's bull-necked mastiff lay behind his chair, curled up and snorting softly. Deana and the boys, exhausted from their ordeal, had gone to bed, and the vaqueros, including the old *segundo* and cook, Fernando Sandoval, had drifted off to the bunkhouse.

"You know, Senor Fargo, you may stay on here as long as you like," the don said, staring at his cigar coal as he and Fargo sat at a small, wrought-iron table under an orange tree. "My house is large and, I have to tell you, lonely at times."

"I appreciate the offer," Fargo said. "But I'm going to take Deana and the boys back to Kansas."

The don smiled and canted his head on his spindly shoulders. "Ah, Senorita Dixon. A fine-looking young woman. A serious, polite young woman, as well. High-bred. If I may be so bold, I am not sure you should let her get away."

Fargo drew on his cigar and blew the smoke over the low adobe wall to his right. "Foolish move, I admit. Problem is, I'm just not ready to settle down yet."

The don regarded Fargo bemusedly through the heavy smoke cloud wafting around his head. "Maybe you will change your mind on your way to Kansas."

Fargo laughed and stubbed out his cigar in the ashtray. "Maybe, but I doubt it." He laughed again to cover his regret. "Reckon I'll be heading to bed. Thanks again for your hospitality, not to mention springing me from that tight spot in the hills."

"I am just glad we were riding through that section of country," said the don, turning away to stare into the dark yard beyond the wall. "The frontier would not be the same without you."

Fargo headed for the inside door. In the open doorway, he stopped and turned back to the don, sitting by the wall and staring pensively into the darkness beyond. The Trailsman didn't say anything for a few seconds, measuring his words, not sure he should voice them. It pained him that he'd had to kill that gracious man's daughter.

"You must feel some regret . . . knowing she's dead?"

Don de la Garza turned toward him, a philosophical expression on his gaunt, tired face. "No more regret than I would feel after the death of a rogue wolf put down after decimating my herds. *Buenas noches*, Senor Fargo. Sleep well."

Fargo turned through the doorway, climbed a set of stairs, traversed a dark hall, and opened the door of his room. Inside, a lamp was lit. Deana stood beside it, facing a large window open to the fresh night breeze, her back to him. She was naked, her slender back flaring to hips burnished delectably by the flickering lamplight. Her hands were raised, holding her hair in a loose pile atop her head.

"What are you doing here?" Fargo said, tossing his hat on a table. "I thought you were tired."

She turned. "I was, but then I started thinking about you." As she dropped her hands, her gold-blond hair fell about her shoulders, framing her cream breasts.

She moved toward him and wrapped her arms around his neck, pressing her breasts against his chest, the nipples prodding his shirt. She looked up at him, frowning.

"How did you get into that hotel, anyway, Skye . . . and learn which room I was in?"

Fargo's heart skipped a beat. He placed his hands on her slender shoulders and leaned down. "Secret of the trade, my dear."

As she opened her mouth to respond, he kissed her, pulling her tight against him and running his hands down her long, smooth back.

She pulled her head away from his, wrinkling her forehead. "But . . ."

He closed his mouth over hers once more, picked her up, carried her over to the bed, and collapsed on top of her.

A minute later, the only sounds escaping her mouth were sighs of passion.

LOOKING FORWARD!
The following is the opening
section from the next novel in the exciting
Trailsman series from Signet:

THE TRAILSMAN #309
CALIFORNIA CARNAGE

California, 1858—
where the stagecoaches that run
along the Old Mission Trail
carry trouble for the Trailsman.

The swift patter of footsteps along the street told the
big man in buckskins something was wrong. He stood
in the shadows of an alley mouth with his lake blue
eyes narrowed, waiting to see what was going to
happen.

The girl came out into the night. Her long brown
hair whipped around her shoulders as she jerked her
head back and forth to look for any sign of her pursu-
ers. She was on the far side of the street from the
man in the shadows, but he could see her fairly well in
the light that spilled through the doorways of several
cantinas, still open at this late hour.

From somewhere in the darkness, a man stepped out in front of the fleeing girl. She skidded to an abrupt halt and cast wild glances around her, looking for somewhere else to run.

Before she could move, the man came toward her, his arms outstretched. She opened her mouth to scream. It was a hot, muggy night in the pueblo of Los Angeles, a night for screaming.

But before she could make a sound, the man clapped a rough hand over her mouth and grabbed her arm with his other hand. Cruel fingers dug into the flesh.

"I've got the bitch," he called to whoever had been pursuing the girl. Their hurried steps came closer.

Across the street, Skye Fargo strode out of the shadows and said, "Let her go."

His voice was deep, powerful, and carried well even though he didn't raise it. The man holding the girl rasped a curse and swung around, pulling her with him so that she was between him and Fargo.

"Who the hell—"

"I said let her go," Fargo repeated as he continued across the street in an unhurried fashion. He was a muscular man, a little above medium height, bigger than he appeared to be at first glance, with the speed and power of a wolf rather than the bulk of a bull. A short, dark beard sprouted on his jaw, and intelligent eyes peered out from under the broad brim of a sand-colored hat.

"What business is it of yours?" the man who held the girl challenged. "Better light a shuck out of here, hombre, before you wind up in trouble."

A faint smile touched Fargo's lips. "I don't think I'm all that worried by threats from a low-down skunk who manhandles girls."

"You son of a bitch. You don't know who this little bitch is—"

At that moment, the girl sank her teeth into the palm of the hand over her mouth.

The man screeched in pain, jerked his hand away, and hauled her around so that she faced him. Blood covered the palm of the hand she had bitten as he raised it to smash it across her face.

The blow never landed because Fargo had never stopped moving, and a couple of quick steps brought him in reach while the man was pulling his arm back to strike. Fargo's right fist shot out in a short, sharp punch that smashed into the man's face. The man let go of the girl as he stumbled backward. He caught his balance and clawed at the butt of the gun stuck behind his belt.

Fargo didn't give him a chance to pull the weapon. He bored in, fast and hard, sinking a left in the man's belly. Whiskey-laden breath gusted out of the man's mouth. Fargo threw a right cross that clipped him on the chin, and followed that with a looping left that landed with solid impact on the jaw. The man went to his knees and then toppled onto his side. He lay there gasping for breath and groaning in a soft voice.

Fargo stepped back and turned as he heard a rush of footsteps behind him. The man's friends had caught up.

The Colt in Fargo's hand rose as he came around to face the others. They stopped short as they saw the black mouth of the gun's muzzle pointing at them. The heavy revolver was rock-steady.

"Move over here behind me," he told the girl, who was staring at the man Fargo had knocked down. She did as he said, scurrying to put him between her and the men who had been chasing her.

Three of them glared at Fargo in the dim light. Like their friend, they were roughly dressed, beard-stubbled hardcases, the sort of no-accounts who could be found in the saloons and whorehouses of any frontier town. One of them demanded, "What the hell did you do to Elam?"

Another of the men said, "Better put that gun down, mister, before somebody gets hurt."

"It'll be you who does," Fargo said.

"Damn it, there's three of us and one of you, and we're armed, too!"

"That means I'll kill two before any of you get off a shot. The third man *might* be able to hit me, but I'll kill him, too, before I go down."

From the grim, worried looks on their faces, none of them doubted what Fargo said.

"Hell, take the little slut, and good riddance," one of the men said. "We don't want her that bad. And after you've been saddled with her for a while, you won't, either. She's nothin' but trouble."

Fargo heard the angry hiss of the girl's indrawn breath behind him, but he didn't look around, didn't take his attention off the men he held at bay with his Colt. "I'll take my chances," he said. "Now pick up your friend and get out of here."

"You're gonna be damn sorry you ever laid eyes on us, mister."

"Too late. I already am."

Fargo moved back to give them some room as they came forward to help the first man onto his feet. He was groggy but conscious enough to stand under his own power once they got him upright. He glared at Fargo and might have tried to attack him again if one of his friends hadn't pulled on his sleeve and said, "Let's go, Elam. It's over."

"No, it ain't," Elam rumbled. "It ain't hardly over."

But he left anyway, moving off in an unsteady walk, accompanied by the other three men. Fargo didn't lower his gun until they disappeared in the darkness down the street, and even then he didn't holster the weapon.

"Mister, I can't thank you enough—" the girl began.

Fargo turned to her and grasped her arm with his free hand. His touch was gentle compared to that of the man who had grabbed her before. His voice held a note of urgency, though, as he said, "I don't trust those varmints. Let's get off the street before they double back and try to bushwhack us."

She gasped. "You think they would?"

"They might." Fargo steered her toward one of the nearby cantinas. "We'll be safe enough in there, where it's light."

He had at least one friend there, too, because the place was run by a man named Pablo Almendovar, whose life had been saved by Fargo several years earlier. In fact, Fargo had been headed for Pablo's cantina when he'd heard the hurrying footsteps and his instincts told him trouble was about to emerge from the darkness.

He'd been right about that. Over the long, eventful years he had learned to trust his instincts, and they had seldom betrayed him.

The atmosphere inside the cantina was close and smoky despite the open door. Not much air stirred tonight. Half a dozen men stood at the bar, drinking, while another half-dozen were scattered at the rough tables. In one corner, an old man strummed a guitar. His blind eyes gazed out at the room, and what they saw, only he knew.

The massive man behind the bar had a wild tangle of black hair and a jutting beard. His dark eyes lit up as he noticed Fargo. "Skye! Welcome, *mi amigo*, welcome!" His gaze moved to the girl beside Fargo, and his bushy eyebrows rose in appreciation.

Fargo holstered his gun and headed for one of the

empty tables, signaling to Pablo to bring drinks. He held a chair for the girl, then sat down opposite her. In the smoky light from the cantina's lamps, he saw that she was older than he had taken her for, around twenty years old, more of a young woman than a girl.

And, although she was dressed in a long, colorfully embroidered skirt and a low-cut, short-sleeved white blouse that left her shoulders bare, the sort of outfit that the Mexican girls here in Los Angeles wore, she was not Mexican. Her clothes and her long dark hair had made her appear otherwise in the dim light outside.

But her eyes were light blue and her skin was fair and creamy. Her heritage might be pure Spanish, but there was no Indio blood in her. Fargo wondered if she belonged to one of the old Californio families, the Spaniards who had ruled California before it became part of the United States a dozen years earlier.

"Thank you," she said in unaccented English. "I don't know what would have happened if you hadn't helped me."

"Nothing good, I'd wager," Fargo said. "I reckon introductions are in order. My name is Skye Fargo."

No other series packs this much heat!

THE TRAILSMAN

**Available wherever books are sold or at
penguin.com**

National Bestselling Author
RALPH COMPTON